I0744504

The Magic of Ordinary Things

12 TALES OF WONDER, MAGIC, AND THE HUMAN EXPERIENCE IN ORDINARY AND EXTRAORDINARY WORLDS

LISA S. SILVERTHORNE

Death's Other Cousin

The Keeper of Dreams must show his cousin, Death he understands human love. Or give up being Dreamkeeper.

The Delicatessen from Beyond the Monolith

A troubled young cop has premonitions about shooting his partner. He'll break the rules of time and space to prevent it.

Permanent Ink

A goddess-turned-tattoo artist is caught between two worlds where only love can free her.

Speechless in Seattle

A young man's stuttering breaks the spell that will make him a full wizard, causing magical chaos in Seattle. Will he fix the magic and claim his power?

Starfish at Ebbtide

The Sentinels stand silent watch as a young woman struggles to make the biggest decision of her life. Changing everything with one wish.

Introduction

Magic is all around us. In the unlikeliest of places, in unexpected things, ordinary things, and it appears at the strangest moments. Sometimes, it's a hushed magic with resonance that we barely notice when it arrives. A fox trotting across the backyard. A twenty dollar bill in an old wallet. A shooting star across the night sky. Coincidence? Maybe. Opportune? Most definitely.

But magic? I say a resounding yes!

Quiet little magics that make us believe in a better world. And our world needs magic more than ever. It needs those soft tugs on our heart strings. It needs the hope of finding just the right thing when you need it most. And when you wish upon that star in the dead of night, desperate for it to be granted, the sight of that shooting star might make the difference between hope and giving up.

And sometimes, in the midst of the darkest, bleakest night, the most extreme pain, or crippling fear in the face of extraordinary violence, that gentle whisper of magic can be all that keeps us together. It's a comforting push against the dark. A tiny protection against evil. A silent whisper of hope when all but a glimmer has fled.

In this collection, you will meet flawed people, broken people. People in their worst possible moments—who've chosen that moment to shine. And even people that thrive on darkness.

All of them share one thing: that need for hope, some of it false and some of it true. And within that quiet shimmer of hope, *the magic of ordinary things*.

Lisa Silverthorne
Las Vegas, Nevada
October 19, 2022

Death's Other Cousin

Even if you're not Death, January's still the best time to visit nursing homes, retirement centers, and the elderly. With the holiday rush over, much of the world just settles back into its familiar routine and coasts for a while. Out of habit or sheer exhaustion, I'm not sure, but either way, everything just sort of takes a deep breath and chills the fuck out, making it easier for me to make my rounds and confer with my cousins. Visit the world's oldest residents and do my thing.

So, Cousin Death asked us to meet him outside the Cedar Hill Manor retirement community. Set on a rolling meadow of thick green grass, willow trees, and wildflowers, this place looked like a grand dame in a summer parade. The sprawling, gabled Victorian rest home, with ice-blue cypress siding trimmed in white with fish scale shingles, two turrets, a slate roof, wraparound porch, and spandrels everywhere. A line of wooden rockers and Adirondack chairs overlooked the hibernating hydrangeas, velvety hollyhocks, lavender, and lilacs waiting for spring. It looked like a dream.

Hell, I wanna retire here! I'd volunteer to be the social programs director and everything. Organize outings and picnics...dreams would practically take care of themselves in this place. Only an occasional need for nightmares to even things out, keep people in line.

See, I got smart this year. This time, I negotiated a warmer start with my oldest cousin. Northern California (up from a balmy -18° C in Lavrentiya, Russia). I know, I know—those people's dreams are important, too, but I needed a change of district.

I check my watch. Almost 8 P.M. Right on time. Sky's dark except for the deep magenta blush along the horizon. Sun's already set in this part of the globe, dropping like a golf ball in a sand trap (Cousin Death sucks at golf).

I pull in a big, deep breath and stretch my arms wide, taking in the crispness. The sweet, clear air. I do a little spin, working my legs and feet, holding in an urge to sing a few lines of *California Dreamin'*. Air's fresher than a hundred of those pine tree air fresheners hanging in the car. Cool and refreshing, unlike that stuffy, dark gothic manor Death calls his crib (I call it a mausoleum).

Wind kicks up, blowing across the rolling meadow, rattling the branches of tall Cedar trees and Douglas Firs that frame the property. I let the air rush over me, grateful it isn't full of chemicals—enough to get my cousin's attention. Which isn't good for anybody these days.

Sorry for not introducing myself all proper like. I'm Death's other cousin, Cousin Le and I handle dreams. No, I'm not that fat slob, Sleep. Always stretched out on somebody's sofa, sleepin' off a bribe or takin' a nap instead of helping out his cousins. Or helping mortals with insomnia—some cat too grumpy to sleep. Animals dream too, ya know.

No, I'm the taller cousin. The taller, younger, charming, and devastatingly handsome cousin that handles mortal dreams and nightmares.

That's right, dreaming is my business. Dreams are important, people! They're not just some fluffy distraction for your brain. Or wasting time until the real thinking begins.

Hey, I save lives and protect people! Like sending Little Billy some cute, fuzzy dinosaurs to dream about after his lunk-head older brother leaves up images of gunshot victims on his computer.

C'mon, the kid's only four years old!

Look! It's William (or Cousin Death as he's known in the profession), standing on the porch, looking fly in his black robe, hood arranged neatly around his shoulders. His scythe shines with fresh polish, its gnarled handle smooth as he clutches it in his right hand. And those shoes. Shiniest black leather I ever saw…damned expensive, too. Ferragamo's? Berluti?

I can't hold back my frown. He looks a little thin, those mahogany brown eyes colder than I remember. His brown hair's a little shorter than usual. And straighter. He's about three inches shorter than me and at least twenty pounds lighter. I wave and shuffle toward the porch.

His face brightens a little when he sees me and smiles, holding out his hand.

"Leo, Happy New Year." His voice sounds tired. No, jaded. This isn't good.

Normally, he enjoys his job. Likes bringing people over, striking down people being bastards, and showing the nice ones Act Two of their own stories. He's good at it, too. Can scare the shit out of hardened criminals, have them pissing themselves in terror and then gently carry kids and delicate old ladies across to the next shore.

William glances around, the sky filling with stars. "Dammit, where's Fred?"

"Cousin Lamont and Cousin Kayla should be on their way," I offered. East Coasters are always late. Can't help it. Time zones are a bitch.

William shakes his head, propping his left hand on his hip. "No, Leo, they're not. This meeting is just you and me." He grimaces. "And Fred. But he's probably passed out on a couch in Vegas."

A Russian chill brushes across my face and I shiver. A private meeting with Cousin Death? That isn't on my list of things to do today. I'm feeling really unnerved right about now. Something ain't right.

"What's up, Cousin?" I ask, stepping onto the porch, the wind cool at my back.

Damn, that scythe looks awfully sharp tonight, but William always talk straight to me.

"Leo, we have a problem," William says with a deep sigh and leans against his scythe.

"Hey, you just say the word and I'm all over it," I say, holding out my hands. "Whatever it is, I'll fix it. Okay?"

Then William gets all quiet, sighing a couple times as he paces across the creaky porch. And it's gettin' really dark out here. Colder, too.

Dammit! And Fred's out there sleeping away, napping, and having a grand ol' time.

William presses his hand to his forehead, frowning now. "They want me to retire you, Leo."

"What? Retire me? But why?" It's so much worse than I'm thinking. This is bad. Real bad.

"Your dreams are boring, Leo," says William with another sigh. He reaches out and lays a hand on my shoulder, squeezing. "They're not what mortals want anymore."

I begin to shake. Boring? Not what they want? That's a stab in the chest. I turn away from him, staring out across the meadow. Dreams are all I know. They're a part of me. How can they be...boring?

"Leo," he says in a tired voice. "You've been in this business for so long, but you've forgotten how the other side feels. How they think."

His grip on my shoulder tightens and I feel him pull in a deep breath. Winding up for the pitch.

"You've forgotten about love, Leo," says William in a soft, deadly voice. "Something that all of us dream about it."

That was more than a curveball. Or a third strike. It's a hollow point to my heart. Blowing through valves and muscle. Ripping through arteries and splattering my life force all over the celestial walls of the profession. William never misses—with scythe or words. And when he says that his other cousin has lost his touch, he means it. Leo, Death's Other Cousin of Dreams doesn't know how to love anymore.

Shaking and out of breath, I drop down on the wooden steps, feeling heavy and useless. I half expect to see William and his scythe dribble my beating heart all over the wraparound porch. I've been at this dream thing a long time. I'm good at easing pain and fear, at building confidence, even taking braggarts down a peg or two.

But love...wow...maybe he's right?

"What happens now?" I ask him in a quiet voice.

"You've got until midnight tomorrow," says William. "Show these people how to love, Leo. Make it happen."

When I get to my feet, Cousin Death is gone. Nervous, I stare at the white door leading into the retirement home. Twenty-four or so hours isn't much time. I have my work cut out for me. But this is important.

Hell, these people need something to hope for, something to dream about.

Taking a deep breath, I step through the closed door (being a cousin has *some* perks) to find some students to learn about dreams. And hopefully a few teachers.

I FEEL LOST, OVERWHELMED WHEN I ENTER THIS RETIREMENT home and I try to appear as human and as mortal as possible. Like them, I was young once. Twenty-two when I joined the business, so I let them see the real me. Jeans, grey tennis shoes, Cardinals baseball shirt, and red hoodie.

The place is huge! It smells like lemons with a hint of bleach and fried fish. A big, sprawling family room with shiny hardwood floors and lots of windows letting in the sunlight on all sides of the room until those floors sparkled. Overstuffed chairs in deep blue and sofas in soft greys and greens fill the space, occupied by lots of seniors, but most of them stare into the distance, looking lost against the warm sand-colored walls trimmed with white crown molding. Coffee tables and end tables in rich cherry wood are scattered throughout the room, unused, clear glass lamps dark but casting little sunlight rainbows across the wood floor.

It looks more like a photo shoot or a furniture store. It doesn't look lived in either. It feels kinda empty even though there's a constant stream of elderly people tottering in and out of the room, canes, and walkers creaking. Some are tall and bony with pure white hair and others thick bodied and hair speckled grey. Others roll into the room in scooters or wheelchairs and others plod in on their own. Only one or two have some younger family members in tow. And grandchildren buzzin' around like dragonflies.

I cast a little tendril of excitement through the space as I stir up memories of past dreams.

Conversations spark through the room. The people almost seem content, smiling and laughing. A stocky old woman with short white hair and soft brown eyes watches me as I sit down in a chair. Two younger kids, seven or eight, bounce around her wheelchair, chasing each other. Like grandma was just a post between them. I look closer. Their mother, about my age, motions at her kids with a cell phone smashed against her right ear. Babbling away to someone. Then I realize she's the granddaughter and her kids are the great-grandchildren.

My gaze meets the old woman's. For just a moment, I see her sadness. The corners of her mouth turn up, happy because someone has noticed her. But then she looks away, folding her age-spotted hands in her lap.

A shadow darts through the room. I glance up, frowning.

Fred. Asleep on the couch beside the woman's wheelchair. Bastard. Catching some Z's while I'm fighting to stay in the business. And grandma looks like she hasn't slept in days. I want to scream at him, make him do his job.

Instead, I get to my feet and wander over to the old woman and her granddaughter. About five feet four, the young woman with reddish brown hair and hazel eyes that gleam almost gold in the light as she stares past her grandma. She looks like she weighs about a hundred pounds. And she talks so fast into her phone that I can't keep up with the conversation. There's a thick gold ring with a ruby on her thumb. The two boys are playing tag now, running around their great-grandmother like she's a piece of fucking furniture.

And I'm the one who doesn't know how to love? These people all need a class on the subject.

I step between the darting kids, past their chattering mother, and sit down on the coffee table in front of the old woman.

"Good evening," I say, offering her a smile. "I'm Leo."

The old woman's eyes flutter open, staring at me a little wide-eyed. Like she's not used to being noticed. She smiles. "Good evening, I'm an Aries."

I laugh at her joke. "Actually, I think I'm a Scorpio."

"Are you visiting someone, Leo?" she asks, running her fingers through her white hair.

"A few people," I say, returning her smile. "Now, I've decided to visit you."

"I'm Helen," she says.

"Of Troy?" I ask. "Have those thousand ships launched yet?"

She laughs, her cheeks smudged pink now.

While her granddaughter chatters away on her phone, Helen and I talk about her life and how she came to Cedar Hill.

"Jim and I met in London in1942. I was stationed there, part of the Women's Army Corps." She laughs and her brown eyes sparkle like something lit them from the inside. "Drove ambulances and smuggled supplies."

I grin. "Wow, you drove an ambulance?"

No foolin'! I'm totally impressed. When I was nineteen, what— three years ago—I still had trouble driving a stick shift. And this woman, at nineteen, probably drove one all over England and France. While being shot at.

"Gigi drove an ambulance?" the older boy says, blue eyes wide, his gaze on his grandmother.

Gigi? Oh, I get it. GG, great-grandmother.

"That's how I met your great-grandfather," she says with a wink at her granddaughter who doesn't even notice.

"Tell us, Gigi! Tell us!" shouts the younger boy, those big brown eyes as big as planets.

Both boys huddle against the coffee table, watching their great-grandmother talk about dodging machine gun fire in the ambulance. Her face flushes, eyes filling with emotion as her memories (and her past) come to life. Her body shifts, almost pulsing with energy until I half-expect her whole body to sparkle.

Her grandkids look mesmerized, eyes filled with wonder, every word she says touching them with excitement and curiosity.

"And I held my breath," she says, exaggerating a big breath with both hands, her voice soft and intense. "I just knew that Nazi soldier was gonna look up at any moment and see me pressed up against the side of the truck."

Helen's grandkids move to either side of her wheelchair, each leaning on the armrest, eyes focused on her.

"Then what happened?" asks one of the boys.

"Jim and I crawled through the grass on our bellies until we got past the guard post," Helen continues, brown eyes wide, her voice sweeping and dramatic.

"Did the Nazis see you?"

Helen shakes her head, silvery white curls settling around her face. She's grinning like a banshee now. "Nope. I got Jim back on his feet, letting him lean on me until we made it to the ambulance." Her gaze shifts to me. "When we got past the guard post, Jim leaned down and pressed his lips against my ear. He said that if we made it back to the field hospital in one piece, he was gonna marry me."

A shiver rushes across my skin, my eyes stinging a little. Damn allergies acting up.

"Did he propose?" I ask. Hey, even I like a happy ending. I let the cousins downstairs handle the nightmares.

But I already know the answer. It burns like a flame behind her watery brown eyes. Helen wipes back tears, nodding.

"I drove him back to the field hospital and they swarmed over him, treating wounds and broken bones." Helen reaches over and lays her left hand on top of mine. This gal's as sweet as pie. "The next morning, when I sat down at his bedside, he took my hand in his and slid this onto my ring finger." She points to the sparkler on her left hand and it's still a beauty. Just like Helen. "Helen Louise Parker, will you be my driver for the rest of our lives?"

Her voice catches in her throat, trembling now, but the faraway look in those bright brown eyes is a million miles away. With Jim. In a dream, I let trickle from my hand to hers.

Finally, she looks up at me. "And that beautiful Englishman, the love of my soul—he said that he wanted to ride beside me for all the rest of his days. And that's just what he did."

Tears slip down my face and I cry with her. I see the images, but I haven't let myself feel them for a long time.

"Thank you, Leo," she says, patting my hand, tears funneling down her face. "For the next 70 years—even if it's only in a dream." She leans against my shoulder, her voice softer now. "If I could go back and drive him around for another 70 years, I'd do it all over again."

She will. In her dreams. And I'll see to it. Damned allergies!

"Leo, let me tell you about my rose garden," she says and I grip her hand.

So many dreams! They all bunch together into a tangle of emotions that push down my spine and through my chest. She tells me how the weeks bud into green leaves and stretch into long, willowy tendrils of months then years that climb across trellises, past the window, and onto the porch, maturing into full blooms. Years then decades. A lifetime of springs and winters. Until that one last sleep under the winter snow. But see, the blanket of snow's too cold and heavy and it stays too long. And when spring finally warms the ground and melts the snow, there's only blackened thorns and leaves. And the memory of those full, fragrant blooms.

Helen's story moves me like a Mac truck jackknifing on I-5.

"For now, these two young'uns keep me busy," says Helen with a deep sigh, hugging her great-grandkids to her chest. "Another part of my Jim that still goes on."

I look over at Helen's granddaughter, phone smashed against her ear. I can't help rolling my eyes. So oblivious. Missing some of the best moments in her life. She needs to put down that phone and live her life.

Helen nods at her granddaughter. "Don't be too hard on Tara, Leo. Being a single mother's hard enough even before the accident—"

"Accident?" I ask, frowning.

Helen smiles through teary eyes and pats her granddaughter on the hip. "Right now, Tara's takin' care of her mother, my daughter. There was a terrible car accident." Her voice falls to a sharp whisper. "Her dad didn't make it. That's his ring on her thumb."

I feel a massive spike of guilt drill through my breastbone and pin my heart against my shoulder blade, exploding in a rolling wave of guilt.

"She's talking to her former high school crush," says Helen. Again, Helen's face brightens, a smile on her face. "He was driving the ambulance the night of her parents' accident. He's an EMT studying to be a doctor."

My whole body is a pile of jelly now, overwhelmed by the emotions surrounding me. And history repeating itself.

Okay, who the hell's cutting onions while my allergies act up? That you, William?

I get to my feet and hug Helen. "Thank you," I say in a choked half-whisper.

"Thank you," she says.

I reach over to Tara and squeeze her shoulder. She glances over at me and nods.

Turning around, I take in the sea of faces throughout the room. Nurses. Patients. Residents. Family and friends. In each face, there's a story. About people they love. People they've lost. And in each pair of eyes, memories and emotions churn, ready to surface at the first kindness shown to them.

And behind those memories are dreams.

Dreams are my business. But for so long, I've made those dreams safe, sanding down corners and softening emotions so nothing hurt, nothing cut, and nobody bled. I hid the scary dreams. Muted the angry dreams. Protected everyone from the hurt and pain when they dreamed about people they lost. People who died.

Those dreams have to get through. They have to continue. Just as they are.

Once more, I look around the room, looking into every person's face, realizing that the one thing I no longer see is a stranger.

Well, okay—there's still Fred sprawled out on one of the couches, snoring his ass off. Stranger than anyone else I know. The room dims and William walks through the closed door, still in his robes, still carrying that scythe.

"You're a quick learner, Leo," he says, patting me on the back. "Thought you'd have to get through half the room before you understood."

I reach up and squeeze his hand. He returns my gesture and I feel the warmth of family against my palm. In my heart. Feels good.

"My protection was hurting people, I get that now," I reply, bowing my head.

William nods. "I look forward to seeing how their dreams change. Here and everywhere else."

He meets my gaze and holds it, one last moment of warmth until that hollow fragileness returns to his eyes. But just for an instant, I see the pain of that burden in his grey eyes. And then it's gone. Cousin

William, always the professional, but I feel the chill of that responsibility dance across my heart. And I'm glad I just handle dreams.

William is back on the job again.

In the reflection of his scythe, I see a blond-haired man in an olive military uniform, holding a red rose in front of him. Waiting. I gasp. Jim!

"So soon for Helen?" I ask, wincing.

William shakes his head. "Not right away, but soon."

My muscles go slack, feeling relief. I have time to craft some wonderful dreams for Helen. And Tara. I'm not going to waste this chance to heal. And love.

A loud, rasping snore draws William's attention to Fred.

Fucking Fred, sleeping away on the couch. He jolts up from the couch, his snores rattling him awake. With hooded lids, he stumbles around until he's standing beside William.

"Cousin," he says to William in a sleepy voice. "How are you?"

"Working. And you? Dreaming of your next assignment?"

"Hey, that's my job!" I shout.

Fred glances at me. "Cousin Leo," he says, nodding. His attention snaps back to William. "Say, about that—where exactly is Lavrentiya? Minnesota?"

I hold in a laugh. "It's on the beach, Fred," I say. "Balmy weather—you'll love it!"

It's the first time I've seen Cousin Death laugh out loud in years. Fucking Fred.

CHALK BOMBS EXPLODED ACROSS THE CROWDED, SMALL-town street festival, startling Ava Harris. Through the haze of purple
and turquoise smoke, she saw him. Standing beneath the street-lights. At the festival's entrance.

Searching for her? Her stomach somersaulted, dropping into her feet.

She froze, the night muggy and sticky against her skin. Five years of pain and healing rushed back. Gary Burke was back in Indiana. She shuddered. Back in Sapphire.

Why? To terrorize her for testifying against him? Sending him to prison?

Her heart raced, fight-or-flight screaming flight. For a moment, she couldn't breathe.

Five years ago, he'd gotten a decade in prison after raping and almost killing her in an alley during Sapphire's Starlight festival. Before Burke, the festival had been her favorite part of summer. She'd intended to reclaim the hometown festival for herself tonight.

Until Burke showed up.

Without so much as a text to warn her.

She backed away, puffs of orange and yellow and red chalk clouds rising in her wake, desperate to fade into the crowd. She had to find a way out of here.

Scent of fresh-cut grass was sweet against the smell of hot asphalt and sunscreen as she moved deeper into the crowd, bursts of colored chalk filling the expanse.

The street dance was starting. Behind her. At the other end of the street.

Ava turned, slipping through the rabbit warren-like holes in the crowd and ran.

Before he saw her.

Sandals clapped against pavement, her breath ragged, fear twisting the old knots in her stomach and bubbling up the memo ries she'd tried to bury.

No, it wasn't supposed to be like this! After five years struggling back to normal (whatever that was now), this was her night. Her hometown. Her recovery.

Local police assured her she'd be notified when he was released from prison. That she'd be the first to know. That he'd be arrested if he came near her.

Didn't someone know he was here? Back in Sapphire like nothing happened. Like no one remembered what he'd done to her.

That he was a monster.

The Indiana heat wrapped around her like a wool coat. Stifling. Sweltering. Taking her breath.

She swiped at her face, bangs trickling purple and blue rivulets down the sides of her face, onto her pink tank top, jean shorts damp and clinging to her legs.

Thunk!

Ava jumped.

Another burst of chalk, yellow and green, misted the hot night with colored smoke.

She glanced around for a safe spot, gold lights twinkling overhead, expecting him to be right there. At six-two, he'd towered almost a foot over her, long thin face twisted and leering, stony brown eyes wild.

She shuddered, pulling in a breath. A chill rippled across her skin, turning it to gooseflesh, the memories still so visceral that they ached through her.

Big, sweaty hands like embers against her skin, tearing off her halter top, pushing up her skirt as she fought. Kicking and clawing. Screaming. The sweet stink of Jovan musk cloying against alcohol and sulfurous bad breath as he smashed a clammy hand over her mouth. And whispered in her ear.

I'll kill you if you fight me.

Those overpowering, muscular arms like anacondas choking the fight out of her as he ripped off her panties.

Forcing her to submit.

Shaking, Ava glanced back toward the streetlight at the corner of Main and River Streets, to keep him in sight. In front of her so she could escape.

A cold wind blew across her heart. Gone.

She bolted between two embracing couples dusted in layers of colored chalk, sandals scraping pavement. Her breaths came in hot gulps, triple-digit heat still battling the night and cool sliver of moonlight rising above the Wabash River.

Weaving in and out of the crowd, she struggled to hold back the panic and fear.

Why had he chosen her? Why?

The cops treated her like a suspect that night, insisting on knowing what she'd worn to the festival. As if a miniskirt and halter top at a hot summer street dance was just asking to be assaulted.

Like it was her fault she'd been raped. Like she'd somehow asked for it.

The one exception had been a handsome blond Sapphire cop who rode with her in the ambulance that night, holding her hand. He'd given her the only safety she'd known that night. Before the numbness set in and claimed the rest of her emotions. Her parents had been out of the country on business, leaving her to face all of it alone. But Officer Hawk Davis stayed by her side through the whole ordeal, through the investigation, arrest, and trial. She'd gotten to know him. To care about him—and maybe something more.

Until the sentencing.

Then he just vanished from town without a word. She never saw him again. She never got to thank him for being there. Or to find out if she'd just been another assignment.

Ahead, she rushed beneath the gold lights twinkling under swaths of gossamer fabric draped in arches across the street that ran behind the hardware store and in front of the row of ginger bread artisan shops facing the Wabash River Walk. A winding trail ran parallel to the river and the street.

She'd managed to finish her counseling degree, but it took five years to come back to the festival she loved. To face her demons and take back her sense of security. To stir awake that scalded sense of joy the lights and plumes of colored smoke once brought.

She shuddered, glancing through the crowd at the alley that cut between artisan shops.

Where that monster had dragged her, with a huge crowd of people right there, oblivious to the assault.

No! She balled her hands into fists. She wouldn't let him shove the memory of that night back into her head. She wouldn't relive it again.

Fairy lights glimmered along the shops' gabled roofs, reflecting off the dark river water like Monet's water lilies. Softening her panic.

She took a breath. Held it. Released.

Each store, painted a pastel color and trimmed in white, had their doors open wide and candles flickering in the windows. Pottery and paintings. Wool scarves and woodworking. Ceramics and jewelry sparkling against the warm haze of candles and lights.

Every summer, people came to the festival from all over the state, swelling Sapphire to three times its size. Indiana's best-kept summer secret.

Like Gary Burke's release from prison.

Past the shops, dozens of people gathered under the fabric arches and twinkling lights as stars appeared in the humid night sky. They used to shut the lights off downtown to see the stars better, but they stopped five years ago.

The street dance was starting.

Relieved, Ava pressed into the closeness of the dance crowd. There was safety in numbers.

The band, four bearded guys in shorts and ragged T-shirts, began to play, drums thumping as a steel guitar whined a tinny melody that gave way to guitars thrumming their best Southern rock anthem into the sultry night.

The crowd cheered and sang along as more chalk bombs hissed through the thick heat, settling against sunbaked asphalt and people dancing in the flush of colored chalk dust. Sidewalks steamed against the tangle of swear-slicked bodies flailing in the wash of colors.

Fury burned through Ava's flushed face, splattered vivid blue and purple, throb of bass echoing beneath the frenetic drumbeat swirling the crowd into a frenzy of sweat and bodies and classic rock, everyone moving together as one. Ava tried, but all she wanted now was to scrunch flat and fold herself into the sea of faces that Gary Burke didn't recognize.

Colored chalk dust clung to her dark hair and face as a comforting mask. Maybe it would keep her out of that monster's reach?

Breathe, Ava. Just breathe.

Tang of cold beer mixed with the smell of sweat and chalk and hot pavement. The triple-digit heat had barely cooled as she glanced up at the stars filling the night sky. Wanting to wish on them again. To look ahead in her life instead of always looking back. Except for Officer Davis. She couldn't get him out of her head. What happened to him? Did he leave the area? Moved to the big city? Found a wife? She'd asked about him around town, but got no response.

Lightning bugs flickered in the dark, rising like bonfire embers as fairy lights twinkled against the translucent fabric arches.

In front of the alley.

Fear spiked cold through her chest, the ghosts of that night rising as she glanced around the dim lit street. Through the tangle of people dancing and clapping. In the sweltering heat burning her face as the bass riffed out "Bad to the Bone."

She surveyed the festival's perimeter again. Sidewalks. Sawhorses blocking off the street. Grey-and-white beer tent at the end of the block. Rush of the Wabash whispering through the short bursts of silence.

That's when she saw it.

Flash of stringy black hair. Long, lean shadow twisting across the street. Stretching toward the band.

Burke!

In dark pants and a long-sleeved dark shirt. Tapping his foot to the music as he leaned against a trash can. Staring into the crowd with empty eyes like a shark stalking seals.

Heart pounded against breastbone. Mouth went dry, hands shaking—the old fear rising.

Ava moved with the other dancers, sliding close, folding herself into the dark pockets deep within the crowd.

Don't give away your location, her sweltering brain screamed as she danced deeper into the crowd, moving away from the band.

She crouched. Head down. Around her, feet thumped the steamy asphalt to the beat. Cicadas chirred a steady buzz above the music and the din of the crowd.

Someone grabbed her arm.

The scream bubbled up, but she swallowed it back as the hand clapped gently against her shoulder. She closed her eyes, recoiling, willing Burke away from her.

"Ava Harris," said the buttery-warm voice. "I'm here to protect you."

As her breathing slowed, she opened her eyes, turning to stare at the man at her shoulder.

Her heart fluttered, then skipped two beats.

Hot enough to evaporate the words right off her lips. Sweltering enough to melt a bra clasp in fifteen seconds. Officer Hawk Davis. The cop from the ambulance. Back in Sapphire?

He was out of uniform, in tight jeans, checkered Vans, and a black muscle shirt. He had the body of a surfer, his curly, summer blond hair, crooked smile, and devastating blue eyes hotter than River Street in August. Much more attractive than she remembered.

For a moment, she almost forgot about Gary Burke. Almost. "It's...you," she said, grabbing hold of his arms, feeling that stab of attraction sparking inside again.

Did he feel it, too, or was she just another job to do?

Hawk's smile was bright, but distant.

"Ava," he repeated in that low, warm voice. "Been searching all over Sapphire for you. Glad I found you."

She shook her head, the memory of his kind face and sizzling blue eyes coming back to her from the ambulance ride. So patient. Staying beside her at the trial. And the sentencing.

"You remember me?" he asked above the music and the crowd, a hand on his chest.

"Of course, I remember you," said Ava, her voice sounding small and shaky. "And your kindness. Why are you here?"

"To catch a monster," he snapped.

Her stomach dropped. "He's here. I just saw him."

Hawk moved closer, the emotion leaving his face. Hawk's gaze flitted through the crowd, around the edges of the street dance.

"Burke told his cellmate that when he got out, he'd return to Sapphire to finish the job. Lawyer got him early release on some trial loophole."" His gaze returned to her face, the corners of his mouth flattening into a straight, determined line. "I'm here to close it."

Ava winced, the old sour fear washing over her again. Five years of watching over her shoulder, looking for egress at every party, in every restaurant and every store. Five years of jumping at every unexpected touch.

From anyone. Including Hawk five years ago. Back then she'd been so sure he was as attracted to her as she had been him. Throughout the case and the trial, he kept his distance, except for his eyes. Until he just disappeared. Like he'd never been in her life at all.

"Is it me he wants?" Ava asked, voice quivering, a sudden chill against her skin.

Hawk nodded. "He's a serial rapist and worse, but you're the first woman to testify and send him to prison."

"Why haven't the others testified?" Ava asked, wide-eyed, watching the detective's eyes for emotion.

Hawk's eyes were blue flames. "Because the rest of them are missing. We just haven't found the bodies yet."

The hair on Ava's neck stood up. She pulled in a breath. "He's close, detective," she answered in a shaky voice as he leaned in closer to hear her. "I saw him at the festival entrance.

I'm afraid to leave. Thought the street dance would be the safest place."

"It's Hawk, remember," said Hawk, with those beautiful pale blue eyes and crooked smile making her a little dizzy.

Of course, she remembered.

Ava watched a hint of pain wash across his eyes. "I tried to contact you," she said. "After the trial was over, but you never—"

"Don't worry," he said, ignoring her statement. "There are under-cover cops all over the festival. The moment Burke gets near you, we'll take him down. You have my word."

So, she'd have to see him again. Up close. The thought nauseated her.

But Hawk's determined gaze and confidence burned in the summer heat, sweat-soaked bangs pressed against his forehead, face damp with sweat and flecked with colored chalk as he stepped closer. She trusted this man with her life. And she wanted him in her life like he'd been five years ago.

"I won't leave your side," he said, flashing that crooked smile again. "You have my word."

Ava nodded. "Thank you."

But there was something in the way he looked at her, just a little longer, a little deeper.

"Let's blend into the crowd," said Hawk, and he began to dance beside her.

Dancing with a cop. She smiled, hoping his proximity kept Burke away.

She exhaled, letting some of her fear and apprehension dissipate as she swayed beside Hawk. She tried to focus her attention on him, but with Burke out there, her skin crawled.

How many other cops danced or stood nearby? Watching.

Waiting. Maybe their presence would keep her safe?

"You have a nice smile, Ava Harris," said Hawk, a grin on his face. "It's nice to finally see it."

"Thanks," she said, her smile widening into a grin.

It was nice of Hawk to notice.

"Why did you disappear right after the sentencing?" she asked. The grin faded from his face, a far off expression replacing it, his eyes darkening.

"I got called back to–other cases," he said, his voice unconvincing.

Had he gotten too close? Stepped over the line? She sighed. *Like she had.*

As they danced beside each other, she watched Hawk's gaze still on the crowd, focusing on the perimeter, on people moving around them. Then he'd glance at her and smile, his gaze flitting around the perimeter again. Always on watch.

His focus made Ava relax a bit, feeling that little hint of safety again. Like she didn't have to be on guard with Hawk on watch again.

Abruptly, the band's lead singer announced an old So's ballad. Something from a band called Meatloaf Meatloaf—really? Two out of Three something or other.

A keyboard plinked out a soprano opening, sad and haunting until the lead singer picked up the melody, lamenting about his dying relationship.

People in the audience sang along as the ballad rolled across the muggy street. They coupled up and slow danced together. Some held up their phones, pale blue lights twinkling like starlight against the slow rhythm.

Hawk slid his arms around her, pulling her close, tight against his bare shoulder. He smelled warm like leather. Safe like cedar. God, she remembered how good he smelled.

Stay in character, she told herself, but his closeness and intoxicating scent left her knees a little weak, the song taking her back to her first high school dance and the boy that broke her heart that summer.

And that night in the ambulance.

She'd been terrified of being touched, but around Hawk, something just—let go inside her. Pushed back the trauma and fear of five years, blurring her focus on Hawk. And the feelings she'd buried after he disappeared.

She swayed with him, his body against hers, his clean-shaven face soft against her cheek. The deep rumble of his voice as he sang along was hotter than the state fair in August. God, she'd missed the heat of another body against hers, the gentleness of someone just wanting to feel connected. People shouted out the ballad's haunting lyrics, but

Hawk singing them in her ear made her sink deeper into his warmth and comfort, lose herself in his arms. But even now, at the back of her memory, the cloying sweet stench of musk drowned out any other smell. She'd hated the stink of it, gagging her that night in the alley.

"Is this just part of the job?" she whispered in Hawk's ear.

He lifted his face from her shoulder, his eyes sad now. "Not this time," he said, brushing colored powder off her cheek.

He gripped her shoulders, staring so deeply into her eyes that she thought he might see past the damage and into her soul, but something else played across his eyes.

Pain. He was reliving something that cut him deep. Something that had scarred him as deeply as her own ordeal.

She enfolded him in her arms, wanting to comfort him like he'd done for her.

"I left suddenly, I know," he said, laying his head against her shoulder, his face hot against her bare skin. A soul-rattling sigh escaped his lips as his gaze returned to Ava, his eyes wet with tears. "See, my sister—"

The first *pop, pop, pop* rang out like firecrackers. Like fireworks.

It took several moments to register even as Hawk's body stiffened against the first loud bang. Already moving into action.

He pulled her down, underneath him, against the hot, oily blacktop that gouged her knees and smelled like tar.

Only when the string of sounds pealed above the band a second time did Ava realize they were gunshots.

Around them, people screamed, running and darting like frogs on an interstate. The band dropped down behind the stage, huddling behind amplifiers and cases.

Hawk sheltered her, gun drawn as he scanned for the shooter. "Stay down!" Hawk shouted, waving his arm at the dissipating crowd. "Stay down!"

People fled in all directions.

Something whizzed past Ava's face, almost grazing her nose. With the crowd out of the way, Hawk pivoted, finding a clear line of sight to the shooter. Still protecting her, he returned fire. Toward the dark image crouched beside a trash can.

Hawk covered her again as a hail of shots crackled across the street.

Piercing squeal of police sirens drowned out the screams and the running.

A dark figure lurched onto the street, rifle slung over one shoulder, pistol in his hand. He passed under the gossamer fabric arches, lights flickering against his hard, lined face.

Disappearing into the clouds of colored smoke. Hawk turned.

Out of the haze, a pistol lowered to his chest, firing off three rounds. All three struck Hawk in the chest.

Whump, whump, whump! Like a sack of potatoes hitting the pavement.

Hawk fell backward. Into the street.

"Hawk!" Ava cried, sliding toward him. "Hawk! You can't be dead —please!"

Arms shot around her, throwing her into a headlock, dragging her backward. Out of the street.

"Miss me, baby?" Burke sneered, smashing his rough, unshaven face against hers in a savage kiss.

The sweet stench of Jovan musk made her gag as he dragged her toward the alley.

She fought. Struggled. Kicked and gouged at his face.

He just laughed. An overconfident, acerbic sound that made her skin crawl.

"That should keep all those fucking cops busy for a while," Burke said with a grin. "Now; you're gonna pay for my prison time, you little bitch. And this time, they'll never find your body. Just like your cop boyfriend's little sister."

"What?" Ava cried, wide-eyed, struggling against Burke's hold. "You think he's here for you?" Burke shouted, laughter

rumbling through his chest as he hauled Ava deeper into the alley that ran north, halfway through town.

Far from any help.

"He was just using you as bait. Telling you there were cops out here protecting you. Bullshit! It was only him! He's the only one who returned fire."

Her head swam. Was that true? Is that all Hawk wanted here tonight? To bait the man who killed his sister?

And now; he was probably lying dead in the street. Her eyes filled with tears, the sickness rising.

Burke slung her like a rag doll into the red-brick alley wall caked with chewing gum, spray paint, and dirt. Bricks gouged her legs and arms. The stench of sour beer and urine mixed with the heat and stink of his musk cologne.

She gagged again.

He leaned back against the other wall, pistol pointed down ward as the wail of sirens and screams swirled through Sapphire's dark streets.

Ava bolted, lurching left, sandals smacking the squishy alleyway floor. She pumped her legs hard, trying to get some distance from him.

"Goddammit, stop!"

She shifted out of Burke's reach, shoulders rolling right, and hit the sidewalk on Lafayette Street (in front of the hardware store) running for her life.

An ambulance whined from the distant interstate, moving closer.

Ava tried to make it around the block, but Burke was faster, cutting her off before she got to First Street.

Grabbing her hair, he jerked her backward, dragging her by hair and arm. Back into the alley.

With police on both sides of the alley, turning the street dance into a blockade, Burke tore open her tank top.

No! Her brain screamed. She wouldn't be his victim a second time. He moved toward her, rifle at his back, pistol in his right hand. She backed away until the brick walk was at her back.

He leered at her, grin twisting his thin, angular features until his brown eyes turned cold. Stony.

Her life meant nothing to him. She saw it in the blank, almost bored stare of his eyes. Empty.

He motioned at her with the barrel of his pistol. "Take it all off or I'll beat it off you."

With slow, shaking fingers, she took hold of her torn tank top and slid it off, revealing her black sports bra underneath.

Burke shoved her into the wall again. "All of it! Now!" Rustle of footsteps whispered all around them.

Burke turned toward the sound as she twisted the tank top in her hands. Stretching it long and thin.

Taut.

A shout echoed through the alley, rising in layers. Faint flutter of sobs reverberated from the street somewhere behind her.

She took a step toward him.

Burke still looked toward River Street.

Another step, a smile rising above her fear. Her rage.

Shadows rushed past the alley. Where the street dance had been. Burke lifted the pistol toward the sounds.

She was close enough to see his cold, hateful eyes. Smell his sour, alcohol-laced breath. Hear the sharp hiss of breath as his nostrils flared, teeth grinding as the rage ignited inside him again.

He whirled around, leveled the pistol at her chest. "Burke!" Someone shouted.

He twisted left, toward the voice, shoulders hunching as he aimed the pistol toward the voice.

With a swift, fluid stretch, Ava wrapped the stretched-out tank top around his neck and yanked it tight.

Twisting. Pulling. Garroting.

Shadows rushed down the alley toward her, rustle of metal against fabric, shoe soles crackling against the damp alleyway as Ava pulled the tank top tighter until the monster dropped to his knees, face paper white and gasping.

Someone grabbed the gun from Burke's hand, but she held on tight, not giving him one more chance to destroy her.

The warm palm sizzled against her bare shoulder. Hawk's face swung into view. Her eyes stung. Back from the dead!

"It's over now," he said in a soft, comforting voice, Burke's pistol in his fist.

She kept her grip tight until Hawk's hands enfolded the tops of hers, his voice soft in her ear.

"Let it go, Ava," he said in a half-whisper, buttery voice soothing. "You're better than him."

When Hawk's warm cedar scent punched through the musk and her rage, she eased her grip on the twisted fabric around Gary Burke's neck.

Burke fell forward and Hawk pounced on him with handcuffs. Another officer then another was on the scene, one taking the rifle off Burke's shoulder.

As consciousness returned, Burke's gaze swiveled back to Ava, the hatred in his eyes renewed.

"Never again," said Ava, glaring down at him.

On his knees, he looked small and angry and pointless. She crossed her arms over her chest and stood her ground. She would never let anyone take from her what this monster took. Never again.

As the officers marched Burke out of the alley and into a police car, Hawk returned to Ava's side.

Gently, he took off his tank top and slid it over her head.

Instead of bare chest, she saw the bulletproof vest he'd worn. "I thought you were dead," she said, voice shaky.

That crooked smile burned through her as he patted the vest. "Had to protect you any way I could."

"What about the people at the dance?" Ava demanded. They mattered, too. "Were they just collateral damage to you?"

He shook his head. "Of course not! No one knew he'd shoot up the place. There are lots of injuries, but no one died tonight."

"What about your sister?"

His expression darkened, eyes misting as sweat beaded his face. "Was I the bait, Hawk?"

She had to know.

His eyes widened and he shook his head. "Bait? No way I'd use you as bait to smoke out a killer. Much less a monster like Burke. I came here to protect you, Ava. You're the reason I'm back in Sapphire."

"Burke said—"

His eyes narrowed. "He was taunting you, Ava! Like he's been taunting me from prison, emailing me about my sister. Mentioning the clothes she was wearing. The necklace. Hinting at where he buried her."

Hawk fell silent, his blue eyes shiny in the soft wash of moon light overhead.

"Is that why you—"

"Left Sapphire?" he said, reaching out to brush a purple-caked strand of hair out of Ava's eyes. "I went to Indy. Where they found her burned-out car and purse." His voice hitched. "I had to go."

Ava slid her hand into his and squeezed. "I didn't know, Hawk. Why didn't you tell me?"

He put his hand over hers. "You didn't need that image in your head," he said with a sigh. "Not with everything else you were dealing with."

"Was Burke lying?" she asked.

"I checked out his taunts," he said, his voice catching, turning shaky. "Nothing but old riverbed. I won't stop looking, though. Someday, I'll bring her home to Sapphire."

Ava slid her arms around his waist, hugging his body into hers. Into his warm, soothing scent. She put her hand in his, squeezing.

"Let me hold your hand this time, Hawk," she whispered against his ear, her lips brushing his downy soft earlobe. "It's my turn."

He smiled, turning his body into hers. "I'd like that, Ava." Leaning down, he found her mouth and pressed his lips to hers.

She kissed him back, knowing he'd be at her side when this hot summer faded to autumn and beyond. Into next year's Starlight festival. For now, she'd be at his side, settling into the heat of his embrace. Safe like cedar.

Moonfall

SPACEPORT AMERICA
Sierra, New Mexico

"ORBITAL INSERTION SUCCESSFUL. BOOSTER SEPARATION complete. Heat shields active," Senior Research and Development Engineer, Jack Morgan announced, swiveling his chair around in the small, brightly lit control room.

Cassandra Bailey sat beside Jack in the back of three rows of desks that faced two wall-mounted 120" screens in the windowless, trapezoidal control room where she and her team had camped since the orbiter reached Io, a moment they'd anticipated for a decade. A green Data Frontiers banner, lettered in crisp, white Helvetica, hung on the wall of the control room and lab space leased from Spaceport America, New Mexico's commercial spaceport.

She gripped the edge of the black desk, staring at the large, front screens that shifted from static to black as she awaited connection to the data-collector bot. She was exhausted, eyes watering, but her wrinkled khakis and green Data Frontiers polo made it obvious that she'd slept at the office last night. And not very well. The soft, dull thrum of computers softened the room's palpable silence, scent of old coffee mixing with sweat and a hint of aftershave. She glanced at Jack who sat to her right and then around the room at the rest of her team: four men and two women. This mission was the culmination of her career. She had to get it right.

"Status check on DOV," Cass replied.

"DOV's instruments are online. Dropping heat shields. Initiating first braking bum," said Jack, his deep, velvety voice filling the painfully quiet room. He wore a blue striped dress shirt and khakis, two-day's beard shadow on his sun-washed skin. "She's decelerating within acceptable parameters. Moonfall in nineteen minutes sixteen seconds."

Cass let out a breath, clenching her eyes closed against the assault of data and readings rolling past on her workstation's three monitors.

"C'mon, DOV," Cass whispered. "You've got to make it to Io."

Everything was riding on this moonfall. Everything.

"Nervous, Cass?" Jack asked as he leaned back in his chair, hands on the keyboard, his handsome face illuminated by a row of monitors.

"Terrified," she said in a half-whisper.

"Don't trust your team?" he asked, that dangerous dimple punctuating his smirk.

With that shaggy black hair and large, moon-bright grey eyes, Jack was still devastatingly handsome at forty-five. They hadn't been together for over ten years, yet she still found him attractive.

Cass snorted at him. "I followed you from California to Quebec to Russia and back again, Jack, until you took this job. I let you hand-pick the team. And I've spent every day including Christmases and birthdays with all of you for the past ten years. I think we're way beyond trust here."

Jack Morgan was a god in the industry. At twenty-five, he had degrees from Purdue, MIT, and CalTech. At twenty-nine, he was a Senior Design Lead, on the JPL fast track to becoming a mission director when Cass entered his team as a baby engineer. She became his right hand professionally and personally until their messy breakup. She left JPL (with a broken heart) for Lockheed Martin, engineering unmanned crafts that delivered payloads to the International Space Station. Later, she worked for SpaceX while pursuing her PhD at

CalTech. Her dissertation led her to New Mexico and her own commercial startup.

Cass threw herself body and soul into every aspect of Data Frontiers, securing funding, building a team, and securing essential industry partnerships. She hadn't come up for air and thought about life outside of work since she was sixteen. At forty, she'd finally learned to trust her skills and instincts, but she couldn't help wondering what her life might have been like if she'd thrown as much effort into her private life as she had her career. Would she and Jack have stayed together?

Despite their history, Jack was still the first person she courted for this project. They were both too much alike, but he was the only person she trusted to head the bot's prototyping and rigorous testing.

"That was a joke, Cass," Jack said in a soft voice, those grey eyes intense now. Concerned. She knew that look. "Your sense of humor always goes numb when you don't get enough sleep. You okay?"

She nodded, looking at her hands. She'd kept her distance from him whenever possible, but that had been impossible over the last year. Cass hated to admit it, but he'd stirred up her emotions these past few months, that old attraction awakening again.

"Yeah, the night on my office couch was anything but restful." He raised an eyebrow. "You slept here last night?"

"Wanted to finish studying the data from those last simulations Cortez built."

"Moonfall in sixteen minutes forty-nine seconds," said Sundeep Subramaniam in a thick Indian accent. His hair was bushy and straight, warm brown eyes tired and anxious. "Two minutes until thruster's first course correction."

The forty-four-year-old Purdue grad (Jack's roommate) and former space shuttle engineer was damned near a genius and Jack refused to come aboard without him.

Sundeep developed the orbiter and its launch protocols alongside Cass, who'd researched and tested the series of thruster bums required to place DOV and the lander properly. DOV had to get to Io's surface. Like Jack, Cass trusted Sundeep with her life. And DOV's.

"Sixteen minutes," Cass groaned, drumming her fingers on the desk. "That's a lifetime."

"It's a quarter of DOV's lifetime," said developer, Jenny Li, phone in one hand, huge to-go cup of iced tea in the other.

Jenny sat in the second row of desks between developer, Shuying Kwan and robotics engineer, Cortez Davis. Her thick black hair was tied back with a red ribbon and she wore a sleeveless red sundress. She chewed on her straw as she flicked her fingers across her phone's screen.

Quiet and reserved, Shuying Kwan just nodded, her attention on the sparse thread of data coming in from the orbiter. She wore a green Data Frontiers polo and khakis, thick purple glasses framing small brown eyes. Her hair hung in a coarse bob just past her chin.

Jenny and Shuying were two of the most talented developers Cass had ever known.

Both twenty-somethings, Jenny picked up languages like song lyrics and Shuying developed Als as a hobby. DOV's evolutionary algorithms and emergent perceptions were bleeding edge (thanks to Shuying), allowing the little bot to analyze complex inputs, learn from them, and react based on her conclusion.

Systems engineers, Arum Jain and Matt Weldon sat in the front row nearest the huge screens. Arum, Cortez, and Matt could build anything, take it apart and put it back together better than it was before. For fun, they built engines out of paperclips and batteries. Cortez and Arum pushed existing parameters to their limits for the orbiter's high-gain antenna while Matt developed new data compression routines that increased DOV's video and image transfer rates to twelve times current ratios.

Cortez and Matt designed DOV to be small and maneuverable. At six feet tall, DOV had a *head* with an omniscient camera and two *eyes* that were separate camera lenses/video processing systems. DOV's "feet" were six independent wheels with cleated treads and a modified rocker-bogie suspension that gave DOV a 360-tum radius and increased stability to handle Jupiter's wild tidal forces.

DOV's *feminine* triangular torso had five robotic arms (4 articulating and 1 stationary for audio processing) allowing her to perform several simultaneous functions. A well-placed curve (thanks to Cortez) beneath her two camera "sockets" resembled a smile. Jack and Sundeep did everything they could to shield her systems from radiation, giving DOV an hour before Jupiter's radiation belt killed everything.

DOV was the closest thing to a child Cass ever had. She'd overseen the little collection robot's development, helping to shape her ontology and evolutionary algorithms. Cass smiled, remembering nights sitting on the lab floor with Shuying and Jack, cheering as DOV exhibited her first emergent behaviors, like her first words.

They'd witnessed the display of her expressed perceptions, the maturing of her input recognitions, like taking her first steps.

Cass remembered one night in her office, soft white lights glinting off stainless steel cabinets where she sat with legs dangling, Jack sandwiched between her and the wall. He smelled warm with a hint of coconut sunscreen and traces of wood smoke, his shoulder pressed against her like an embrace from long ago.

With her hand on DOV's *shoulder*, Shuying demonstrated DOV's evolving perceptions and learned behaviors.

Cass picked up a canister from the shelf, sending a puff of dust into the air. DOV's robotic arm whirred to life, flicking through the dissipating wisp of dust.

"Composition is seventeen percent plant pollen, ten percent paper fibers, thirty-seven percent human skin cells, twenty-four percent mineral particulates, and twelve percent textile fibers." DOV's female voice was pleasing with soft, bright tones. "Colloquially called dust. Its shape reminds me of a butterfly, Cass. I often wonder how it feels to fly, don't you?"

"DOV!" Cass cried.

"Shuying, that was brilliant," Jack said in a hushed voice, his eyes wide. "Thanks," said Shuying, smiling. "Cass helped me tweak the ontologies. DOV's teaching *us* things now, Jack."

Jack surprised her by pulling her into an embrace. "Weak moment?" Cass whispered in his ear.

"Fond memory," he said. Apparently, he'd forgotten that he broke things off, not her. "Don't you, Cass?" DOV repeated.

Cass touched DOV's extended arm. "Yes, I do, DOV. Like the birds."

"Like a dove?" DOV asked, servos whirring. "I'm named after a bird, aren't I?"

Cass nodded. "Your name's an acronym for Data-collecting Orbital Vehicle." She smiled. "I chose it because I like the image of a dove flying across Io's horizon."

DOV's output responses were the result of emergent learning, moments of artificial intuition-and imagination. They'd just witnessed a level of artificial intelligence once thought impossible.

"Cass?" Jack's hand was on her shoulder, squeezing. Returning her to the present.

"Sorry," Cass said in a quiet voice, her gaze on the blank screen again. "Was just reminiscing. Remember when DOV talked about butterflies?"

Jack nodded. "Wondering how it'd feel to fly? She's flying right now, isn't she? For the first time."

"You're right. I wonder if she's enjoying it. Or if she's afraid. Wish I could see what's happening to her." Cass got quiet, her gaze on the blank screen again. She couldn't help but feel protective of the little bot. "What if I miscalculated something? Missed something."

He rubbed her shoulder. "Cass, you didn't. That's why we're a team. We validate each other's work. DOV will perform like a champ."

"Hope you're right, Jack."

He grinned. "I'm always right."

Sundeep rolled his eyes. "Yes, Jack knows everything, Cass. Just ask him."

Jack chuckled. "Eleven minutes twenty-two seconds. Initiating second braking burn." Cass let out a breath. She hoped the lander survived its landing.

Ten years of development, prototyping, simulations, and AI tweaks to produce DOV, an intelligent data-collection bot. She was the payload aboard a jointly launched orbiter satellite from Spaceport America. Sling-shotting through progressively more distant trajectories from Earth to Mars, Earth to Venus until reaching Jupiter, the orbiter-satellite would inject DOV into Io's orbit and transmit her data back to earth. Io, one of Jupiter's largest moons, was the most volcanically active place in the solar system. With surface temperatures ranging from 3000 degrees Fahrenheit to negative 202 degrees, depending on where you stood, DOV had to stick her landing or this would be the most expensive five-minute mission in history.

Once on Io's surface, DOV would analyze soil samples, gather atmospheric data, map terrain, and stream video/images before conditions eroded her systems. Designed to withstand Io's heat (provided she didn't land in a pit of molten lava), DOV would last about an hour on the moon's surface. Her meticulously constructed evolutionary algorithms would allow her to adapt to new data and learn from it. Testing the AI was just as important as collecting the data.

"Structural temperature outside expected parameters," said Matt. "Matt, check sensors on DOV's outer hull!"

The six foot five, ginger-haired engineer turned his chair toward her, looking apologetic.

"We're still in blackout, Cass."

She cursed under her breath. DOV had to survive. This was the worst wait ever.

"Eleven minutes and thirteen seconds until touchdown," said Jack. Cass sighed. "Thanks, Matt. Keep monitoring it."

She turned to see Jack staring at her, concern in those luminous grey eyes. "Eleven minutes is a lifetime, Jack," she said in a half-whisper.

"Cass." He gripped her shoulders and she stared into his eyes, seeing a flicker from ten years ago. "DOV will survive the moonfall because we designed her to. Remember, she's a prototype. This data will improve our next iteration. What's important is that we'll be getting real-time data from Io, Cass. Io! Even DOV's video and images will be priceless."

Cass was glad that she'd purchased several exabytes of storage space on CalTech's new spectral cluster imaging repository, mirrored through Purdue's fastest research cluster. She nodded and gripped Jack's forearms, remembering long ago nights in his arms. They'd both been so driven back then, so focused on their careers that they didn't have time for anything else. Including each other. Standing here now, she regretted that.

"You're right, Jack. Just think what we could learn from this data. I want this mission to go the full distance."

Nodding, he let go of her. "No matter what happens, Cass, remember that DOV made it to Io. Don't ever forget that."

"Eight minutes, forty-two seconds," Sundeep called out. "I won't," she said and turned back to her keyboard.

"Hull temperature leveling out, Cass," Matt called across the room.

Cass smiled, exchanging a relieved glance with Jack. "Great news, Matt-thanks." The control room was deadly quiet as the countdown crossed the five-minute mark.

Then three.

"Two minutes fifty-one seconds," Jack said.

"Initiating wake-up sequence," said Cass, glancing at DOV's main camera screens. Her stomach clenched as both screens flickered a moment and went dark again. "Two minutes four seconds to moonfall," Jack reported.

"Final course correction in thirty-three seconds," Sundeep announced, wiping sweat from his brow.

"Wake-up sequence received," said Cass, clicking through screens. "Systems initialization and integrity scans in progress."

"One minute forty-one seconds," said Jack, his voice tight.

"AI checks completed," Shuying announced, not looking up from her monitor. "Collection and analysis interfaces are online. Systems scans in progress."

"Hang in there, DOV," Cass whispered through gritted teeth as she clicked through the final initialization sequences and checks. "All systems reporting back as up and functioning. AI uptime twenty-eight seconds and counting. GPS function active. Audio and video feeds responding to integrity checks. Initiating final course correction."

"Fifty-six seconds until touchdown," Jack replied, his voice tense. "Landing gear deployed." He let out a hiss.

"Hull temperature continuing to level out," Matt replied, his voice bright. "Thirty-six seconds," said Jack. He smiled at Cass.

"Almost there," Cass said, returning his smile.

"Landing site coordinates acquired," said Jack. "Deceleration thrusters online.

Activating first decel."

Her heart was racing as static pulsed a staccato rhythm through

DOV's audio feed, black screen flickering as DOV approached the landing site. Her hands trembled when DOV's monitoring UI appeared on her screen.

"Twenty-one seconds," said Jack, his tones clipped, teeth gritted.

DOV was awake now, the end of her blind free fall through Io's atmosphere approaching. Would she stick the landing? Would she even respond back to them?

"Fifteen seconds to touchdown," Sundeep announced as the main screens flickered. "Final course corrections complete. In visual range of landing site."

"Ten seconds to touchdown," said Jack, his voice filling the room. Everyone held their breath.

"Six, five, four..." Jack inhaled sharply. "Three...two...one..." He was grinning now. "Sensors report a perfect four-point landing! Soft as a dove's wing," he announced. "Connection established. Awaiting a response."

The minutes of silence intensified, Cass' chest tight with worry as she glanced at Jack, hating the lag.

The crackle of the audio feed startled her.

"DOV unit responding to status query," said DOV, her voice cheerful. "Connection integrity validated. Data sequencing and collection sensors online and functioning. Solar cells at one hundred percent capacity. Starting video feed. Jupiter is beautiful, Cass. Wish you were here."

"DOV!" Cass cried.

The whole room erupted into shouts and cheers. Sundeep hugged Jenny then Arum as Shuying hugged Matt and Cortez. Cass threw her arms around Jack and he held her tight.

"Congratulations, kid," he whispered in her ear. "We've just made history." She kissed him on the cheek. "Couldn't have done this without you," she said. He nodded. "I *wouldn't* have done this without you."

Soon, DOV's initial readings report echoed through the audio feed.

"Surface pressure averaging **11** bars, temperature approximately negative 198 degrees Fahrenheit. Atmospheric makeup is registering as 87 percent sulfur dioxide. Preliminary surface scan indicates the presence of stable, eight-chain, rhombahedral octasulfur molecules, silicates-

mainly orthopyroxene, and sulfur dioxide frost. Dimensional subsurface-penetrating radar scan in progress."

Everyone gasped when DOV's first view of Io reached the control room. Towering mountains, dusted chalky yellow and drab green, filled their screens. Patches of white sulfur dioxide frost crusted rocks and tops of rises, Jupiter massive on the horizon. The huge, banded planet filled the starry blackness beyond Io. Jupiter's radiation and volcanic heat caused some of the terrain to appear a rusty red, its sulfur molecules stabilized into four-chains. In the distance of the perpetual starry night, massive plumes of fluorescent lava and gas spewed more than a hundred feet into the air, Prometheus, one of Io's largest volcanoes, in the distance.

"It's beautiful," Cass whispered, unable to look away.

"Io must be a geothermic energy goldmine," Jack exclaimed, his gaze unwavering from the screen. "It's ... magnificent!"

DOV pursued data leads and responded to the crew's direction, moving slowly but carefully across Io's terrain. Even when the surface bulged in a sudden one hundred and seven foot incline, DOV didn't flip or topple. Her oversized, sharply treaded wheels kept her balanced and in motion.

"DOV, please review your terrain maps and speculate, based on your data, the origin of any subsurface structures."

"Thanks, Cass," DOV responded. "I'll process that request immediately."

After thirty minutes, surface temperature, Io's sulfur dioxide atmosphere, and Jupiter's radiation took its toll, eroding DOV's shielding and the satellite-orbiter, but her data were still streaming. Sundeep called Jack over to his station and they spoke in whispers with Shuying for several minutes until he returned to his station.

Jack took Cass' hand. "DOV's systems are beginning to degrade, Cass," he said in a quiet voice. "She won't survive another thirty minutes."

"I was afraid of that," said Cass, her throat tight, knowing DOV didn't have long. "Cass, you should see the sulfur plumes," DOV's cheerful voice echoed through the room. "When the dust rises, it's like a cloud of yellow butterflies. See them, Cass? It's beautiful. Jack, I have more data for you concerning Io's Jovian pole reversals. I just captured one of these shifts."

"Thanks, DOV," he responded.

Shuying walked over, her eyes misty behind her glasses as she slid her arms around Cass' shoulders. "This will be the hardest part, Cass. DOV knows that she's deteriorating and will shut down soon. I don't know how her AI will react." She sighed. "Thought you'd want to know."

Cass swallowed hard. "How long?"

"I'm estimating about twenty-four minutes, Cass," said Jack. Cass hugged Shuying. "Thanks," she replied, a lump in her throat.

Over a decade, she'd watched DOV evolve from multiple sets of instructions into a fluid, learning machine and from there, into a questioning entity that had intuition and imagination. Now, Cass would have to watch DOV slowly lose information and functionality.

Die. That was the correct term.

"Cass, you tried to teach me about imagination in the lab once," said DOV, a squawk in her voice processors as the little bot moved over Io's powdery yellow surface.

Slower now.

"I remember," Cass responded. "I taught you to look at pictures of clouds and imagine what their shapes might be. Do you remember?"

Scratchy silence.

"Shielding array has gone offline," Sundeep announced in a quiet voice.

A death knell. Cass bit her lip. The beginning of the end.

Moments of static followed.

"I ... remember, Cass," DOV replied, her speech slowing. "I remember how blue the-sky was that day in Pasadena. As blue as earth from the stars."

Main monitors flickered. Static punching through the audio feed as a picture of Jupiter froze on one monitor, DOV's right camera feed failing.

Warnings scrolled across Cass' screen and she held her breath a moment, remembering that sunny afternoon where she, Jack, and Shuying had taken DOV outside to the cool green grass, smell of lilacs on the breeze, whir and hum of DOV's servos soft as Cass had pointed at a bank of fluffy white clouds floating overhead. Cass smiled, remembering DOV's happy tone as she pointed at the clouds with one robotic arm.

Kittens, she'd said, almost cooing like a child.

Jack snickered until Cass elbowed him quiet while she praised DOV's imagination. "Yes, the clouds were so tall and fluffy that day, weren't they, DOV?"

Jack laughed at me when I said they looked like kittens, do you remember?" DOV asked. "Terrain map of the landing site-completed." Squawks broke up DOV's voice, filling it with static for a moment then faded. "Uploading now."

Cass felt her eyes sting. She glanced at the mission clock. Forty-eight minutes on Io.

She wanted more time. More time for DOV.

"Solar cells at twenty-one percent power," Matt announced. "Twelve minutes of power remaining."

"She's got about ten minutes left, Cass," said Jack.

"I remember, DOV," said Cass, her voice tight as moisture misted her eyes. "But I also remember something *you* said to me that day."

Static filled the room again, video feed still transmitting.

"Tell me, Cass," DOV answered and Cass could have sworn she heard her voice getting slower, thought she heard a whisper of emotion behind DOV's speech.

Must have been her imagination.

Jack slid his arm around Cass' waist and suddenly, Cass felt her knees weaken a little. She held onto the table, still standing as she stared at Io's surface. Through DOV's eyes now.

"You told me you liked your name. I asked you why. Do you remember?" She couldn't stop the quivering in her voice as her emotions spilled all over her words. "You said because doves were soft and sweet and could float free on the air's warm updrafts. You thought humans kept birds so they could momentarily experience flight."

"I remember," said DOV.

"You said birds weren't prisoners though," Cass continued. "They could fly away at any time, but their cage was like a tether, a connection that allowed them to momentarily feel human."

"Solar cells at eighteen percent," said Sundeep. "Nine minutes until shutdown."

Cass swallowed the lump in her throat. "You said I was your tether and you were my dove."

Silence hung in the control room.

"Solar cells critically drained," said Jack in a somber tone. "Ancillary systems shutting down to preserve the core."

"Shuying taught me how to learn," said DOV, her voice markedly softer (weaker?) now. "You taught me how to imagine, Cass. How to perceive. And there were moments when I forgot what I was. Jack and Sundeep gave me wings, but you taught me to fly. How to be human for an hour in a place no human has ever touched before."

Cass clenched her eyes closed, fighting to hold back the emotions.

"And DOV, you taught me how to look past my own programming and focus on the horizon, not on the fact that I didn't have wings. You taught me that fear is a cage with an open door. And sometimes, the biggest impact comes from the smallest gesture."

White noise crackled as DOV's audio channel eroded into garbled stutters, her final video stream cutting in and out, system warnings trilling through the control room.

"Thank you, Shuying and Sundeep. Jack and Cass. I'm–proud to have accomplished our mission on Io. And Cass...I will miss you."

"One minute fourteen seconds to catastrophic power failure," said Jack. He squeezed her shoulder. "Not enough time for a response, Cass. Just one last transmission."

"DOV," said Cass, clearing her throat. "Thank you for reminding me why I became an engineer, why I do this every day."

"Twenty-eight seconds to shut down," Jack said above the scratchy garble of noise as DOV's audio feed dropped.

Cass watched the clock on her computer, biting her lip until the digits changed to mark the passage of a single minute.

The gravelly snarl of static went silent, like a door had just closed. Both mission screens went dark as a palpable silence descended on the control room, the realization inescapable.

DOV was gone.

Cass was surprised when she felt the heavy crush of grief against her chest, tears burning her eyes. She looked over at Jack who was choked up, pain in his eyes. He still had his arm around her waist.

"Data still transmitting," Sundeep announced, his voice barely above a whisper. "DOV completed the terrain map you requested, Cass."

"Put it on screen when it's–down," said Jack.

Cass turned away from the room, walking toward the door, but Jack caught her arm and held it.

"It's okay to feel this way, Cass," said Jack.

She turned to him, staring deep into those luminous grey eyes. At the hurt of losing DOV. Emotions from long ago had stirred to life, reflecting back at her from the depths of his eyes. It wasn't just nostalgia for the good old days.

She couldn't believe it. He still carried that torch.

"This isn't about DOV, is it?" she asked in a half-whisper.

He shook his head, taking her hands in his. "Back at JPL, work broke us apart. I never dreamed that, after all this time, it would bring us back together."

Cass squeezed his hands. "What's changed, Jack? We're both type A's. Both married to our work. What will make it different this time around?"

He smiled, reaching out to brush a lock of hair out of her eyes. "Back then, Cass Bailey was more robot than human, never letting an emotion or weakness stop her from ascending that professional ladder. Back then, Jack Morgan had tunnel vision and could only focus on himself and that Director of Missions placard."

Cass frowned, shaking her head. She started to speak, but Jack laid a finger against her lips.

"Years ago, both of us would have sacrificed a hundred DOVs to bring back ground breaking data." He inhaled sharply. "But tonight, you and I would have given up all of it to bring DOV home from Io."

He pulled his hand away from her face as she let his words sink into her brain. He was right. If there had been any way to bring DOV home, she'd have taken it.

All she could do was nod.

He laid his hand against her cheek, caressing. "If that had been you out there, Cass, I'd have moved heaven and earth—data be damned."

Cass smiled, laying her hand on his. "I'd have never taken that risk."

He grinned, leaning down to kiss her.

"Jack, Cass–terrain map on screen."

They turned toward the main monitor as DOV's terrain map filled the screen. Cass gasped, rushing toward it, Jack behind her.

"Underground tunnels?" Cass replied, pointing at the scans annotated with DOV's data. "Dormant lava shafts?"

DOV's voice filled the room as Sundeep played back her data record. "Dimensional subsurface radar-penetrating scans revealed a network of underground tunnels. Lava chambers ruled out due to the tunnels' distance-and isolation-from volcanic activity. They don't appear to be naturally formed tunnels. They appear purposeful, possibly to harness Io's extensive geothermic energy. Other possibilities could be protection from Jupiter's radiation and tidal effects on the planet's surface. Final assertion: Further study of these tunnels is needed to determine if Io has been visited before."

Jack stared at Cass, that sense of wonder gleaming in his grey eyes, that sense of discovery she'd fallen in love with so many years ago.

"You heard the AI," he said. "Further study recommended." Cass nodded. "Looks like Data Frontiers has a new mission."

"Uh, Cass," he said. "Just before DOV's solars went critical, I made an incremental copy of her AI, capturing all of her change states. All her experiences and discoveries. Her memory."

"So we haven't lost her?" Cass asked with wide eyes.

Jack shook his head. "We'll incorporate it into a DOV II. So she'll remember us and her first trip to Io."

"I'd like that," said Cass, turning toward the monitor.

Another trip to Io, another chance with Jack, and another chance to soar. This time, on her own wings.

Three Breaths

Private Cade Crosby shouted himself awake, the blood-red letters and spirits fading from the nightmare. Breath came in gulps, sweat masking his face and drenching his hair. He sat up in the bedroll, hands against his face, and shuddered in autumn's drizzly mist. In the glow of mealfire embers, South Mountain was a forbidding shadow. Antietam valley below.

But the nightmare persisted. And he felt the weight of impending doom sitting on his chest as he stared out at the watchfires dotting the valley. Tens of thousands of Reb and Union soldiers—brother against brother—waited for dawn. To kill each other.

And he was first on the list. Marked for death by red ink.

Cade had never been superstitious until tonight. When he saw the red ink. He smashed his eyes closed and tried to blot out the night's roster posting. Nailed to the supply wagon. But the image burned through his fevered brain. Enough black ink to list every single member of the 27th Indiana Volunteers. Including two of the three that found Lee's lost dispatch—each man smoking one of the three cigars to celebrate. With the taste of that third cigar still on his lips, Cade knew the red ink was a portent of death. Despite Momma's protective wishbone charm.

Now, Cade's name was the last name on that roster. But like a deceased soldier, his name was written in red ink. Like he was already dead.

Oh, the sergeant apologized over and over, even crossing out Cade's name and writing it anew in black charcoal. But all of the 27th understood the ill omen. And they kept their distance.

How do you apologize to a soldier you just marked for death?

The scent of woodsmoke mixed with musty tent canvas and sweat, onions from last night's mess sweet against the cool, clean rain. Cade shivered, patter of rain soft as he clutched his Springfield rifle against his damp Union blues.

Not even Momma's wishbone charm could save him. Not now.

He ran his fingers over the bleached white wishbone tied with a leather cord around his wrist. It wouldn't be enough to halt the Angel of Death's hand against him.

Sweet scent of cigar smoke haunted him and he froze, the dream rushing back to him.

Sergeant Bloss, Corporal Mitchell, and Cade, standing in a circle. Laughing as they puffed on cigars. Ribbons of white smoke floated like streamers around them as they each held out a cigar and lit papers on fire. General Lee's signature gleamed blood-red on the papers as they burned. Changing to his name as soldiers died by the thousands around them.

"Cade," someone snapped in a sharp whisper. "You all right?"

Cade turned his head, staring at George Murphy, a tall, broad-shouldered farm boy with thick black hair and brown eyes, a sharp contrast to Cade's pale hair and grey eyes. He and George were the same age, volunteering together, leaving behind their family farms in Indiana to fight against the rebs. He hadn't spoken to George since he'd been wounded at Cedar Run.

George dropped down beside him on the bedroll and nudged him with his shoulder, holding out a small flask.

Cade accepted it, taking a swig of rotgut that burned all the way down to his feet.

"Fine. For a dead man walking. Aren't you afraid you'll catch your death sittin' this close to me, George?"

"Stop talking like that," George said in a sharp whisper. "You're a hero like Bloss and Mitchell! Handin' over Lee's battle plan like that. 'Sides, you saved my life at Winchester."

Winchester. His first fight—and the 27th's. Seemed like a lifetime ago. He and George had been terrified.

"You'd have done the same for me, George," Cade said in a half-whisper.

George patted him on the arm. "I even heard Bloss say those cigars were lucky charms. Said they'd make them reb bullets just bounce right off."

Cade ran his hand over his face and took another pull off George's flask. The whisky burned all the way down again. He'd kept the nub of the cigar, wrapped in a handkerchief in the haversack at his side.

Not even Lee's cigars could save him now.

"They wrote my name in red, George," said Cade, sighing as he ran his finger over the smooth white wishbone charm at his wrist. "In dead man's script. It's too late."

What would they tell Momma when it happened? Cade winced. *It'll break her heart.*

He'd scribble out a note before morning to tell her that he loved her and he was sorry that he couldn't come home to her.

George shook him hard and snatched the flask out of his hands. "Fight for it, Cade—like you fought for me at Winchester. Remember?"

Cade nodded at the lanky farm boy, remembering that day with trepidation. But Momma's good luck charm had protected him that day. Helped him save George, too.

"We was surrounded by Jackson's Rebs, remember? Runnin' through the streets of Winchester when they flanked us again."

"So much smoke and chaos," Cade said, "we barely got out that day."

George nodded. "When I got hit, you carried me on your back all the way to Martinsburg." His voice broke and he sucked in a breath. "So, this time, you fight back harder! Even the Angel of Death if you haveta, but don't you give up. You hear me?"

Fight back against such a powerful portent? Against the Angel of

Death? The odds were impossible. Not even Lee's cigars could win a fight with death.

"I'll try," said Cade with a sigh, the hopelessness rising like nausea in the back of his throat, making him gag.

"Do more than try, Cade," George said, patting him on the back. "Pa always said it takes three breaths to beat Death."

"What? Three breaths?" Cade said. *What the hell did that mean?* "George, what are you talking about?"

George grinned, shrugging. "Pa never explained that part to us. Said we'd each know which three they was."

"Not helpful, George," said Cade, frowning.

"Well, think on it a spell, Cade. Maybe it'll come to you in your sleep?"

George stretched and unfolded his lanky frame from the bedroll, leaving Cade alone in the rainy mist collecting along the dark ridge.

Throughout the rainy night, Cade counted the watchfires along the ridge, flickering in the mist like fireflies. He wondered how many soldiers crouched out there, ready to shoot him and his unit.

And where was the Angel of Death? Did it crouch behind him or wait in the shadows along the road to Sharpsburg? Looking for the bold red mark of death that marked Cade's soul?

George's three breaths hung at the edge of his thoughts as the sky lightened and first light approached.

And the battle at Sharpsburg loomed.

In the silent dawn, Cade and the Indiana Volunteers trudged through loamy black cornfields, thick, dry stalks stretching over six feet tall. Hiding barns and sheds and fencerows.

Smoke swirled through the fields as Minié balls hissed past. Splintering dried husks and stalks. Scattering ears of Indian corn. And Cade's company of soldiers.

Flash of grey. Crunch of boots against hard cornstalks.

Cade froze, crouching to tear a cartridge and load his Springfield.

A man to his right fell. One behind him.

Minié balls showered the fields like a hailstorm, battering the rich black soil and pounding the dried-up corn husks to dust as Cade and the others returned fire.

He turned, head down, rifle raised.

Sunlight cut through the clouds, burning off fog. Blood-spattered cornstalks swayed. Percussion shells whistled overhead.

The man to his left cried out. He was dead when he hit the ground.

"Break for the Miller farm! Go!" shouted a sergeant.

Cade broke into a run, his breath coming in gasps. He scanned the cornfield, searching for George. The lanky farm boy moved like a jack rabbit through the field ahead.

He tried to match George's pace, weaving through the field. Crouching behind a fencerow, he huddled behind a post, Minié balls sizzling past in all directions. Gathering his courage, he lurched ahead through tall grasses, into another field of corn, rushing toward the white farmhouse that lay ahead. And the swampy swale surrounding it.

The ground quaked, knocking Cade to the ground as percussion shells ripped open the blue sky. The heavy shells slammed into the fields, chewing up stalks and fencerows—and soldiers. Gouging troughs into the loamy black soil.

Cade crouched behind another fence post, heart racing. Powder dusted his face as he gritted his teeth and tore another cartridge. Smoky scent of sulfur gagged him as he loaded the Springfield again.

Returning fire.

Minié balls scoured the fields around him from all directions. Percussion shells shrieked and wailed like banshees through the clouds, slamming into the ground and shaking the world apart. Parrot guns thundered across the valley, chewing up fences and outbuildings. Muskets and rifles growled across the valley in a steady, deafening roar.

He was alone and pinned down! Miller's farmhouse was just too far away now.

He tamped down the powder and froze. That's when he saw it. It made him feel sick inside, the world closing in on him.

His heart bounced into his throat, pounding his rib cage and chest as panic rose.

The hand reached out to him.

He stumbled backward, rifle raised.

George, face spattered with blood and powder, grabbed his arm and pulled him to his feet, his Springfield clutched against his left side.

"This way, Cade," he shouted above the percussion shells, motioning him along a length of tall grass and into another cornfield. "Hurry!"

"Where's the gun battery?" Cade asked.

"West woods," George answered.

Cade fired off a shot, taking down a charging man in a grey uniform before it got to George.

When had they stopped being people and become just colors to him?

He glanced down at the rebel's face. Clean shaven. Young. God, oh, so young! Sixteen-year-old farm boy at best.

His stomach lurched. He felt sick inside.

"Keep moving, Cade!" George shouted above the roar of musket fire and shoved Cade forward, toward the swampy patch of lowlands known as Mumma's swale. "Battery's just ahead."

They crouched low, following a handful of soldiers through the fields toward Mumma's swale. Passing bodies and so much blood that it made Cade sick.

Somewhere out there, a rebel battery of Parrot guns was destroying union troops. Stolen from a federal battery. The one they had to take control of it.

Would he meet the Angel of Death there?

Among the dried, bloody cornstalks. Or out here somewhere—lost in a sea of grass—or sinking into the swampy muck of the swale ahead? Beside the Parrot gun killing his company of soldiers?

Somehow, he had to stop them.

Cade followed close behind George, heads down as they made their way into the lowlands in the shadow of the Parrot gun that stretched across the field and into the swamp.

A flicker of white caught the sunlight, casting a thin shadow across his left side. Something fluttered, blotting out the sun. Something huge.

George shouted his name.

Cade turned, rifle raised. And fired.

Powder flashed. Orange burst turning smoky as something slammed into his right side. Knocking him to the ground.

His Springfield skittered across the ground and sank into the swale ahead.

Like a bird of prey, a shadow soared above him, great white wings beating the air. Muffling the sounds of battle.

Cade clawed at the broken cornstalks, grabbing for a handhold. He rose on his knees as something murky and dark landed in front of him.

Storm clouds gathered overhead as the entire battlefield slowed to a stop and froze around him.

Is this what it's like to die?

Cade's whole body trembled at the sight of her as the smell of sulfur mixed with coppery death.

Her long, flowing ebony hair coiled around her shoulders, piercing gold eyes without emotion. And armor that was both shadowed and shiny, flowing around her like smoke as she lifted a flaming broadsword over her head.

The Angel of Death. She was here for him.

And he was unarmed.

George's words flooded his brain. *Just three breaths, Cade! What did that mean?*

The fiery sword hissed through the air.

Cade rolled out of the way as the gleaming blade slammed into the ground in front of him.

He slid left, throwing himself backward as the blade cut deep into the earth, parting it like butter.

Scrambling to his feet, he unfastened the wishbone cord from his wrist. His good luck charm. *Would she slice him in two if he tried to use it?*

Cade stood his ground, holding out the wishbone in front of him as the echo of his mother's voice touched his ears. *Carry this close to your heart, Cade,* she'd said and he'd put it on his left wrist. *It will bring luck from my heart to yours.*

Up 'til now, he'd never had a reason to test it.

He took a deep breath and held the wishbone high.

The Angel of Death charged at him, flaming broadsword crackling above her head, the heat reflecting off her spectral armor. Back at him.

The heat of the blade singed his face as it sliced through the air and split the earth at his feet. Flames danced across the dry cornstalks and set the grass alight.

When he couldn't hold in the breath any longer, he exhaled.

The sharp, trembling rush of air turned icy as it engulfed Death's sword. With a flicker of orange, the sword sizzled then went dark in Death's hand.

Knocking her backward nearly a hundred feet into the swampy expanse. The broadsword lay smoldering in the grass.

The Angel of Death staggered up from the ground, surprise pinching her brows. She glared at him, gold eyes narrowing as she picked up the broadsword that no longer burned.

"Love won't save you," she said with a hiss.

"No, but it knocked you on your ass for a bit," said Cade.

She let out a deep guttural scream, swinging the sword in a wide arc above her head.

Cade stumbled backward, falling over broken cornstalks and burnt ears of corn to get clear of the blow.

The polished blade, no longer flaming, glinted as sunlight pierced the heavens, spilling across the dried ground. The world shook as Death's blade sliced a huge furrow into the earth. Like a burrowing animal, it surged across the soil at him. Knocking him to the ground again.

His body hit the ground hard, flying up like a rag doll, and landing on the sharp, broken cornstalks protruding from the rich black soil.

"George!" he shouted. "Could use some help here."

Then he remembered the cigar stub in his haversack, the one he'd smoked with the other soldiers after finding Lee's dropped dispatch wrapped around the cigars.

The three of them had turned in the dispatch, hoping it would help them win this battle.

Death whirled, slamming her blade against the earth again. The raging shift of rocks and dirt shot across the cornfield, smashing into Cade with more force than a wagon pulled by a team of raging bulls. Trampling him in a crush of churning soil and debris.

Clawing at his haversack, Cade fumbled bloodied fingers over cartridges until he felt the silky handkerchief against his scraped and burning fingertips.

Again, the Angel of Death raised the silvery broadsword above her head as Cade struggled to his knees.

He held out the stub of Lee's cigar, the one he'd smoked with Bloss and Mitchell to celebrate a chance to win this battle. But it'd been more than that to the three of them. He pulled in a long, deep breath of air and held it, the cigar stub quivering in his hand.

To them, finding this dispatch meant trying to stop a bloodbath. And thousands of soldiers from dying on both sides.

Cade released the deep breath of air.

The broadsword broke into two pieces, the top half shattering like a broken window.

Shards rained down the Angel of Death, reducing the massive broadsword to little more than short sword. It still had a razor sharp edge that glimmered as threads of light pierced the dark pall of clouds.

A pale gold light illuminated the bloody battlefield, still frozen across the Antietam valley almost to Sharpsburg.

None of this made sense and Cade wondered if he lay dying somewhere on this battlefield, ready to draw his last breath among the living. After all, they'd written his name on the roster in red ink.

Just one more volunteer giving his life in another faceless battle. Win, lose—living, dead—it didn't matter. His was just another name on another roster somewhere. A roster for the dead.

They'd used red ink, so he'd been expected to die here. From the start.

Cade had accepted that.

But not George.

"George, I'm out of breaths," he said, backing away as the Angel of Death advanced toward him.

She lifted the point of the sword above her head and moved toward Cade who kept backing away from her. He dug through his haversack and shoved his hands in his pockets, desperate to find that third breath.

But he had nothing left to fight with. To fight for. Nothing left to give.

"Cade, don't quit on me now!" George's voice echoed in his head.

Cade took another step back, but his foot hit against a wall. He glanced behind him. Mumma's whitewashed barn was at his back. He was out of space.

And time.

The Angel of Death trudged forward, glint of the sharp remnant of sword she held aloft sparkling like a lantern. A look of triumph spread across her pinched face, armor shifting like smoke as Cade pressed his back against the barn.

Only George seemed to think Cade had something in him worth carrying forward. Something that should survive this battle and any roster of the dead. He sighed. Something inside him that was worth fighting Death for. He didn't exactly know what that was. Or how it became a breath of life against the Angel of Death.

But that's when it came to him. He did have one thing left to give. Himself.

Because Death held no power over someone unafraid to die.

Cade pulled in a deep, trembling breath and dropped to his knees as Death loomed over him, sharp sword point hovering above his head.

"I'm not afraid," he whispered and let out a long, satisfying breath.

Like smoke, the Angel of Death dissipated into mist and floated away as the sun beat down on the battlefield. And the crushing reverberation of the battle flooded in, the world turning once more.

But Cade woke up at a field hospital. It was little more than a tent with folding tables and lines of patients that hovered at the edge of the fighting. The air was thick and coppery, a strange chemical smell hanging around him as he looked up from the stretcher.

The doctor stared down at him, white lab coat and apron tinged rusty-brown and smelling of bleach. His brown eyes were intense as he set down the bottle of chloroform, his hands pocked with dried blood.

"You're lucky to be alive, young man," said the doctor in a stern voice. "Takin' out that Reb battery by yourself took a lot of guts!"

Cade frowned, staring up at the doctor. *What battery?* He'd taken on the Angel of Death at George's urging.

"Where's George?" Cade asked. "George Murphy. He's part of the 27th Indiana Volunteers like me. He was with me at the...battery."

The doctor glanced at a brown-haired woman in a white dress holding a bottle of amber liquid in her right hand. The woman shook her head and muttered something Cade couldn't hear as the doctor reached over to a stack of papers and held one out to Cade.

"Here's the 27th's roster, Private Crosby," said the doctor, pointing at the paper.

Cade squinted. It was the same one he'd stared at in camp. With only his name written in red ink.

He looked closer, his eyes widening, stinging as the pain hit him square in the chest. He couldn't breathe as he ran his index finger across the last name on the roster—the only name written in red.

George Murphy. Died at Cedar Run. August 1862.

The Delicatessen from Beyond the Monolith

"CHANCE, WAKE UP! IT'S A NIGHTMARE."

Brittany's voice echoed above the standoff, three men with guns on each other. Gripping my Beretta, I stared down the shadowy figure to my left. To my right, my partner, Gil Boone also leveled his Glock at the shadow man.

"Police! Drop the weapon!" Boone shouted.

The shadow-man flicked his pistol toward Boone, then me.

Silver glint of the shadow man's gun barrel pointed at my chest. Just six feet away. I tried to turn my weapon left, at the shadow man, but I couldn't stop my arm from swiveling right. The 9mm arced toward Boone.

"Chance! What you doin'?" Boone shouted, face pale, southern accent thick. Mouth open, eyes wide, Boone stared at me in shock, his Glock still trained on the shadow man.

I stepped toward Boone, heart hammering my chest as I fought against every inch, every movement. I didn't want to shoot Boone! I wanted to shoot the shadow man. But I couldn't stop it.

Boone backed away from me, footsteps clacking against old linoleum, skittering through trails of dirty moonlight pouring through the deli window.

"Chance, it's me—your partner!"

He thumped a hand against his chest, pistol turned toward me.

I leveled the barrel at Boone's chest. Couldn't pull back, couldn't stop it.

"Dirty cops deserve to die."

His face was Formica-white, pupils blotting away grey irises as my finger slid to the trigger.

"Chance, no!"

With a thunderous bang, time slowed. Flash of orange against smoke.

Boone screamed.

The bullet struck his chest, the sound like thumping an unripe melon, bright red plume spreading across his shirt.

"Chance!" Brittany shook me.

I shot up from the mattress, holding my head and shrugging off Brittany's touch. With clammy fingers, I peeled the St. Jude medallion off my sweat-slicked chest.

"It's okay," she said in a soothing voice, cold hand on my back. "Just a bad dream."

I pulled away. It wasn't just a bad dream. I'd had it every night for over a week.

"Chance, talk to me," she said in that hurt little girl's voice.

At first, it was charming. Now, it made my teeth ache. I got up, grabbing my cell phone.

"Come back to bed."

"Gotta drain the lizard," I muttered, padding toward the bathroom.

I couldn't look at her. Couldn't stand the touch of her hand, the sound of her voice.

She didn't know that I knew she was cheating on me.

Five years on the force had taught me to read people, detect lies, and unravel them. Like Brit's accidental text last Tuesday, telling me how much she loved our Tuesdays together. I worked late, falling into bed after she was asleep. That night, she'd smelled different. Like oranges and cedar. Reminding me of the aftershave she insisted on buying and I'd returned.

Guess she'd found someone else to wear it.

I took a piss, washed my face and hands twice, and went to the living room, counting the hallway floor's creakiest boards as I stepped over them to reach the couch. A purple monstrosity Brit bought. Shivering, I grabbed the forbidden throw off the back of the couch.

The kitchen's microwave read 5:02 A.M. Two hours before my alarm. I didn't want to fall asleep and risk returning to the dream. It always ended the same way.

With me killing my partner.

"Chance," Brittany called in a sultry voice. "Come back to bed."

Brit used to wear all that lacy shit to bed. Or nothing at all. Now, it was a long-sleeved, Hello fuckin' Kitty nightshirt that hung to her knees and those fucking alien sponge curlers in her dark hair, face sticky with some shit Dr. Oz recommended.

Cops weren't easy to live with, either. She complained I was never home, or too tired to go out. When we first met, she was working two jobs and taking night classes. Now, she sometimes worked part-time or took a class, if it didn't interfere with maxing out my credit card.

Was it me? Had I killed her ambitions?

"Chance, please come back to bed," she said, standing by the couch, arms crossed over that damned cat staring at me with maniacal, empty eyes. Her brown hair stuck out by her right ear, brown eyes smudged with black liner. "Really? You're using the decorative throw? Get a blanket out of the ottoman."

"It's bad luck," I muttered.

She rolled her eyes. "That's ridiculous."

"Brit, if I sleep, I'll have the same dream."

Her eyes turned hard, cruel—she despised me. She slapped her hands against her sides, Hello Kitty mocking me. "You're twenty-seven, not seventy! All these routines and rules! God, you're so OCD—just like your father."

I hated when she threw that term around so casually. Had she forgotten how I grew up? Living with a superstitious mother and a father with severe OCD was a nightmare, leaving deep, unhealed wounds. That Brit couldn't resist poking with a sharp stick.

"Do you have any fucking clue what OCD means?" I shouted, sitting up.

"Of course, I do," she snapped.

Dad's Obsessive Compulsive Disorder nearly destroyed my family. Chores were done exactly as he instructed, or we did them again. And again. Once, I spent twelve hours one Saturday scrubbing the kitchen floor because I'd cleaned the tiles out of sequence. Garbage was sacked up in a certain order: cans sorted by type and size, rinsed, and laid side by side; cardboard boxes flattened and placed on the bottom. Every Friday, beds were stripped at precisely five o'clock. Fresh sheets were folded with exact corners, left-hand pillowcase on first, opening facing out, and then the other. Top sheet and comforter were turned down exactly twelve inches at the pillow line. If not, Dad tore everything off the bed and made us do it again.

And again.

"OCD isn't alphabetizing your DVDs and relocking your doors a couple times!" I shouted.

"I'm going back to bed."

Brit stomped off, slamming the bedroom door.

I gripped my St. Jude medallion. My mom insisted the power of Christ could heal Dad. She hid crosses and saints' medallions all over the house for protection, ran from black cats, avoided ladders, and crossed Friday the 13th off the calendar. I wore it for protection. For her.

Maybe it'd protect Boone from me?

WHEN THE ALARM CHIMED AT SEVEN, I SHOWERED AND dressed in jeans and a flannel shirt, Beretta in my side holster. After I'd checked the window and apartment door locks four times, I left for work, came back to make sure, then drove to the precinct.

I couldn't get the dream out of my head. Was it a premonition? Heartburn? Bad pastrami?

My mom claimed that some foods gave people nightmares. Was it possible? I'd had this dream ever since the downtown deli where Boone and I ate every day ran out of roast beef. And tuna salad. Both times, the old guy behind the counter had talked me into pastrami.

Maybe it was the pastrami? I could hear Mom's voice in my head. Or the rumor about Boone going around the station?

———

"Hey, kid," Boone said as I slid into his dark blue Charger and fastened the shoulder belt.

"Hey," I muttered.

He handed me his tablet. "Listen to this tip line call that came in last night. About our armed robbery suspect."

I played the audio.

"I seen the police sketch on the web," said a scratchy voice. *"It's Craig Easton. Old high school bud. Been braggin' about a robbery and throwin' 'round lotsa marked bills. Deals heroin out of the Monolith and Cozy's. Bastard cuts it with cornstarch and baby powder. Hope he burns."*

I handed the tablet back to Boone. "Another reason to get this guy off the street."

"Ran a check on Easton," said Boone, a twang in his voice. "Only one prior. Misdemeanor drug possession."

"We got an address?"

"No," said Boone. "Checked his current and last known. No sign of him."

"Let's head out to the businesses where the marked bills were dropped," I said and picked up the handset as Boone started the car. "Dispatch, this is Detective Sinclair. En route for a walk and talk on Fifth and Main."

The radio beeped as we rolled out of the parking lot.

"Detective Boone," said the dispatcher. *"Got a 10-21 from Delbert Higgins at the Monolith Deli on Fifth and Main. Is that your 10-75, over?"*

Boone frowned. "Roger that, dispatch. 10-77 is about thirty minutes. Over."

"Dispatch out."

"Looks like the Monolith got a marked twenty from last week's armed robbery," I said.

"Delby that new guy?" Boone asked.

I nodded.

Delby was a friendly old man. Always suggesting additions to my sandwiches. To improve the taste of the sandwich and the day. I always turned them down.

Boone settled back in the driver's seat, always calm, collected, and patient. Thin but muscled, five-nine to my five-eleven, with coal black hair to my blond. When I first made detective, the precinct called us Starsky and Hutch because we were so close. When they asked about Boone's wife, they meant me, not Karen.

"Need to wrap this case before Sunday, kid," Boone said as his Charger rumbled through morning traffic, headed toward the Sip n' Fill on Ninth and Ferry.

I rolled my eyes. "If I hear about your vacation one more time, I'm gonna puke."

My stomach twisted into a knot. I hadn't told him about the rumors in the precinct, accusing him of lifting items from evidence lockup and selling them to pay for his vacation. For months, things went missing from evidence shortly after Boone had been there—including several marked bills recovered from the Federal Savings robbery. An investigation had already begun.

He glanced over at me, grinning. "In six days, it'll be warm sand and margaritas for me and the Missus. Wish you could be there, kid."

"Bullshit," I said, laughing. "Karen would divorce your ass. She sees me enough as it is, wouldn't you say?"

He laughed, right turn signal clicking. "She keeps threatening to trade me in for you."

Boone was my best friend. I trusted him with my life. That nightmare made me sick inside.

"You okay?" he asked.

"Fine. Didn't sleep well last night."

He let it go, turning into the Sip n' Fill's parking lot.

By one o'clock, we'd collected all the marked bills and headed to the Monolith Deli. It was fast, good, and close to the precinct.

"What you gonna do if they're out of roast beef, Chance?"

I glared at him.

"It's Monday. Roast beef, right?"

I just shrugged.

Boone smirked, hand against his chin. "Tuesday's turkey and Swiss. Wednesday's pastrami. Thursday's ham and cheese. Friday, tuna salad." He snickered. "Delby gonna ruin your whole day with pastrami again? A piece of lettuce? A smear of mayo?"

Boone loved to make fun of my food routine. I'd stuck to it every single day since we'd become partners. Maybe I'd tell him why someday.

"You gonna arrest him if they're out of onion rolls?" He went quiet as we entered the deli. "I do love those rolls."

The building was circa 1900 with wrought iron accents, marble columns, and big green shades on each window. Its high ceilings were tin and its floors were the original, faded yellow-and-green checked linoleum. Squeaky green booths lined the front window, a few tables scattered through the rest of the room. The black slate lunch counter held an antique brass cash register. Above it, three old blade fans hummed, stirring up the smell of raw onions.

Delby stood smiling behind the counter, white apron tied around his thin waist. He wore a faded yellow dress shirt and tan pants. His hair was bristly short, almost white, face lined, wire-rimmed glasses over dull blue eyes.

"Hello, detectives," he called.

"How you doin', Delby?" I replied, stepping up to the counter.

He leaned his wrinkled hands against the counter, black chalkboard menu behind him.

"What'll ya have?"

"Roast beef sandwich and a soda," I said.

Delby stopped smiling. "Out of roast beef today."

"Not again," I moaned, feeling anxious.

Boone leaned toward Delby. "Kid's got a routine."

The old man slid gloves on and grabbed a sandwich roll, laying it on a sheet of wax paper. "How 'bout pastrami?"

I shook my head, the dream's images coming back to me. "Not today."

"Just cut it fresh not ten minutes ago. It's good for you. Clears the head. Gives ya clarity. And a nice, juicy pickle'll help reflect on the past."

Boone chuckled. "Chance'll have the clarity and reflection sandwich and a soda."

I gave in, not wanting an argument.

Boone and I ate our sandwiches in the corner booth. The pickle wasn't too sour and tasted good with the pastrami, but eating out of sequence unsettled me, as it always did.

I glanced around at the handful of diners, but no one looked like Easton. When we finished, we returned to the counter.

"Delby, we're here about a report of a marked twenty-dollar bill," I said.

"I'll get it," said Delby, opening the antique cash register and handing me a plastic bag. The old style twenty was stained purple, blotting out Andrew Jackson's face.

"Was last Tuesday evening. Security camera picked it up."

"Security camera?" I asked. "I'll need access to that footage."

Delby nodded. "Of course."

Boone's cell phone buzzed, and he stepped back to answer it.

"It's in the office," said Delby, waving at a swinging black door to the left of the counter.

"Kid," Boone said, walking over. "I'm heading down to Cozy's Tavern for a walk and talk."

"Meet you back here?" I asked.

Boone nodded, heading outside and down the block as I followed Delby to the office.

———

THE NARROW ROOM SMELLED STALE AND GREASY. IT WAS just big enough for a small desk and two wooden chairs. A yellowed computer with a CRT monitor sat on the desk.

I showed Delby Easton's mug shot.

He nodded. "Comes in at night. Quiet. Sits in the back booth for hours while people come and go. He was at the counter when I got the marked bill."

I sat in the desk chair as Delby opened the security application.

"Footage files are saved by date," he said. "We'll just test your new reflection talent."

I clicked on last Tuesday's date and a grainy video filled the screen.

"New talent?" I asked.

Delby laughed. "This deli's been around a long, long time. Connected a lot of people along the way. People move in many directions and dimensions along a single line, but when their threads snag or break, knot up like old fishing line, they come through the Monolith, the eye of the needle. And get one chance to untangle or recast it."

I frowned. "With sandwiches?"

"Why not sandwiches?" Delby asked. "Taste good, lots of choices—easy to swallow. People choose their own fixes." The old man winked at me. "I just help 'em a little with the condiments."

I concentrated on the security footage.

"Look back as far as ya like, but it'll only last for the day."

"What lasts for a day?" I asked.

"The pickle," he said and left.

Nothing significant appeared on the footage until around the seven o'clock timestamp. A familiar face entered the deli. I held my breath as he sat down at the counter.

Boone!

Ten minutes later, another man sat down, two stools from Boone. Thinning dark hair, slim build—matched Craig Easton's mug shot.

I gripped the plastic bag with the marked twenty, watching both men order sandwiches and coffee.

Delby laid down receipts, the totals in heavy black ink. Both bills were $7.95.

Both men laid down money. Delby swept it up, marked twenty in hand, but I couldn't see who'd left it.

I ran the video back three and four times, but couldn't see who left the twenty.

In a moment, Delby placed change in front of each man. I paused the footage, staring at the money. Two bills and a coin in front of Easton. Three bills and a coin in front of Boone. My heart bounced into my throat, my stomach turning somersaults.

Change for a twenty.

Boone had laid down the marked bill.

I copied the file to a flash drive and shoved it in my pocket, hurrying out of the office, and past the counter.

"Found something ya didn't like?" Delby asked. "Must have been the pastrami."

I stopped, turning toward him. "Pastrami?"

Delby nodded. "Gives people premonitions."

I rushed outside, trying to clear my head. Did Boone steal those bills out of the lockup? What cop would carry around stolen marked money? Made no sense.

I'd never felt so horrible in my whole life.

Finally, Boone hurried up the block toward me. "Find anything, kid?"

I shook my head. "Made copies to review later."

"Tavern owner IDed Easton in his place," said Boone as we walked up the street toward his car. "Heard Easton tell people to find him at the Monolith. Know what that means?"

I stopped on the Charger's passenger side. "What?"

Boone rubbed his hands together. "Stakeout. Until we have Easton in custody."

I winced and opened the car door, sliding inside.

All the way back to the precinct, I stewed over the security footage, wishing I'd never seen it. How could I turn in my best friend and live with myself afterward? I rubbed my forehead, feeling sick. Wasn't committing my own father to a mental institution enough betrayal for a lifetime?

If I turned Boone in, I'd be an outcast at the precinct. I'd done everything I could to protect him over the past five years, keeping the bad luck and bad karma away. Thought if I just kept it up, kept things steady—in control—no one but me would suffer.

Now, it looked my choices were either turn in Boone—or kill him.

That night, I dreamed about the standoff again. It ended with me shooting Boone. Brit was beside me, an arm around my shoulders. I lay against her until that orange and cedar smell hit me.

I pulled away, grabbing my phone, and headed to the couch. She didn't even follow this time. Not that I'd expected her to anyway.

Counting off the creaky boards, I walked to the couch and stared at the ceiling until my phone alarm got me up and in the shower.

All the way to work, I couldn't stop thinking about the dream. I'd take a look at the deli's security footage. Since I'd be there all day and night.

It was Tuesday. I hoped to fuck Delby hadn't run out of turkey.

With my turkey and Swiss sandwich on the table calming me, I sat in a booth opposite Boone and my laptop all day. I'd worn a scruffy red flannel shirt and my worst jeans. Boone wore jeans and a nice sweater.

"Anything on the security footage?" Boone asked, scratching his jaw.

"Not yet," I mumbled.

Boone set his tablet on the table. "Need some help?"

I tilted the screen away. "I'm almost through."

"Karen wants you and Brittany over for dinner soon. Says she's needin' some girl time with someone else married to the force."

"I'll ask Brit tomorrow. She'll be asleep by the time I get home." After a hard day cheating on me.

I still hadn't confronted her about that text. Part of me wished I'd never seen it, had never found out.

My mom had been with Dad forty years, and never knew he'd cheated. She'd struggled through his severe OCD and two heart surgeries, but when the vascular dementia began, she nearly killed herself trying to care for him. Fresh out of college, I stepped in. In Dad's lucid moments, he told me about the affairs and gave me power of attorney. Then I became the monster that "stole" power of attorney and threw Dad away. After a year, the facility got his OCD and dementia under control. Next month, he'll be released, but I'm not welcome at the house now.

I bit into something mushy in my sandwich

Boone chuckled, setting down his coffee mug.

"What's the matter?"

I held up a slice of bright red tomato with a chunk missing. "Dammit, Delby!"

Delby shuffled over, smiling, white apron around his thin waist, blue shirt and tan pants spotless.

"Need more refills?" he asked, hands against his apron.

Glaring, I held up the tomato. "Didn't I emphasize the word *plain*?"

He patted my shoulder. "Thought you might need a little foresight today, detective."

"What's that mean?"

Delby winked at me. "Eat the tomato and find out."

"Just eat it, Chance," Boone replied. "It's not gonna kill ya."

But it might kill Boone.

I glanced at Delby, now cleaning the lunch counter, and stuffed the tomato into my mouth, washing it down with soda.

The last few bites of my sandwich tasted spicy. I opened the bread, peeling back the cheese and turkey, finding pastrami tucked inside.

"What the fuck?" I muttered.

Delby was messing up my carefully crafted five-year routine. No wonder I was dreaming about shooting Boone.

Boone laughed so hard he nearly snorted coffee. He finished his roast beef and cheddar on an onion roll as I shoved away my plate. I hunched over my laptop as dusk darkened the downtown streets.

I just hoped Easton showed up before Delby poisoned me.

WHEN THE DELI CLOSED AT TEN, I HEADED HOME. BRIT would be pissed about me being on stakeout the rest of the week. The rearview mirror glinted with car lights as I headed up the hill toward the apartment complex.

Something flashed in the mirror. I glanced up. Images flickered across it, grainy, shadowy—like security camera footage.

I blinked, rubbed my eyes, and looked again.

Figures oozed onto the silvered glass. Boone and Easton standing off, guns drawn.

My breath caught.

A car passed me on the hill, brights shining in my face. I squinted, glancing away to avoid its full force. As I crested the hill, red-brick apartment complex in sight, I saw myself entering the grainy scene. Gun drawn, pointing at Easton.

My heart beat into my throat, blood rushing to my temples.

I nearly missed my turn. When I got to my building, I parked my black Civic, turning off the motor. The scene kept rolling across the rearview mirror, Boone and I facing down Easton. The checked linoleum floor and black slate counter placed us in the deli. Then I turned my pistol on Boone.

I tried to look away, but the images kept flowing.

Flash of orange against smoke. Boone falling to his knees. Dark stain spreading across his chest.

I shoved the mirror down and scrambled out of the car.

That hadn't been a dream! I wasn't asleep.

Then I remembered that fucking tomato slice Delby made me eat. Said something about foresight. Had that been a look forward into the future?

I glanced in the side mirror as I locked the car. My apartment appeared. Empty. Furniture gone, only a mattress, a pillow, and that fucking couch throw remained.

Shaking, I pressed my St. Jude medallion to my lips.

The future said Boone would die and Brit would leave me. Everything was out of control and I couldn't stop it.

I checked the car locks four times and went inside, checking all the door and window locks a few times before I fell into bed smelling like pastrami and onions.

And I dreamed about the standoff again. Fucking pastrami.

When I woke up shouting this time, Brit was sound asleep beside me, her phone on the nightstand. The screen lit up with a text message.

Can't wait to see you again, babe. Call me when you can.
Leaning over, I sniffed her hair.
Oranges and cedar.

ALL WEEK, BOONE AND I STAKED OUT THE DELI, BUT EASTON didn't show. By Friday, I was tired and Boone looked miserable. Lunch was my normal tuna salad. As afternoon faded into evening, Boone and I ate supper at the deli. We both wore scrubby jeans, him in a blue striped shirt and me in a black hoodie to hide our shoulder holsters, cell phones, and badges. A trace of Brit's vanilla musk cologne clung to my clothes. She was probably with someone else right now. It hurt. I still cared.

Tonight, I'd confront her. See if anything remained.

Boone stared at my plate. "That's not tuna salad."

I glared at Delby clearing a table, sleeves of his grey shirt rolled up, white apron pristine over grey pants.

"No, it's turkey," I said, loud enough for Delby to hear. "With Colby-Jack, mustard, and a pickle spear. Told him three times I hated mustard and didn't want a pickle, but he insisted."

Delby stepped over to the booth, a stack of plates in his hands. "Pickles to look back at truth. Mustard to speak it." He winked at me. "And that co-jack just might save your life. Has amazing dispersion qualities."

He put the dishes in a tub underneath the counter.

Boone seemed distracted, barely listening.

"Boone, what's up?" I asked, taking a bite of pastrami, the mustard cloying on my tongue. I glared at Delby across the room. What else had he fucking snuck into my sandwich? I took a quick drink of soda to wash the strange tastes away.

"Chance, I feel awful leavin' this case in your lap."

"No worries, man. Reese is working it with me while you're gone. We've got some leads. If you're lucky, we'll make the collar while you're on the beach somewhere."

Boone took a bite of his meatloaf sandwich, chewed, and swallowed.

"This trip means the world to Karen. Been savin' for it since before you were my partner. For years, I worked nights deliverin' pizzas, puttin' every dollar in the bank. We never had a honeymoon, so I felt I owed her somethin' unforgettable after ten years of puttin' up with a cop's life."

I stared at him. "Why didn't you ever tell me that?"

He shrugged and picked up his soda. "Wasn't important, I guess."

I took another bite of turkey, the mustard making my eyes water until I finished the sandwich. For a long time, I stared at the pickle.

"Just eat it already," Boone growled as he finished his sandwich.

With a sigh, I picked up the pickle and ate it, the dill puckering my mouth.

Delby smiled, looking relieved.

I got up from the booth.

"Givin' up on me already?" Boone asked, a twinkle in his grey eyes.

"I want to look at more camera footage, in case I missed something."

A bell on the deli's glass door jingled, two older women entering as I leaned over the counter.

"Delby, I need another look at the camera footage."

"Help yourself," he said, turning back to the counter.

<hr>

BACK IN THE STUFFY OFFICE, I CLICKED THROUGH SEVERAL days of footage but returned to last Tuesday. I ran it back and forward until it stopped, hoping the outcome would change somehow.

I slammed my fist against the desk. No, this wasn't true! Boone wouldn't do this. Somehow, I had to prove it.

I studied the list of video footage, named by date. Then I saw a file at the bottom of the list, its name starting with a z—like someone had accidentally renamed it.

It had last Tuesday's date! A part I hadn't viewed.

It began with Delby laying down change for Easton, and then Boone stepped out of the frame for a moment. I held my breath, but he quickly returned to his seat. After that, nothing else changed, the two men still eating.

Finally, Delby walked back to the counter. Reaching down, he switched the change, moving the three bills and coin in front of Easton and putting the two bills and coin in front of Boone. He'd mixed them up!

I couldn't stop grinning as Boone pocketed his change and left. Easton remained a while longer, then picked up his change and left.

Boone was innocent. He hadn't taken anything from lockup. And I had Easton on tape passing a marked bill.

I copied the file to my flash drive and rushed out of the office. A shout stopped me mid-stride. I dropped to a crouch.

"Let him go, Easton!" Boone's voice.

Easton, wearing a grubby sweatshirt and dirty jeans, held a .357 Magnum to Delby's head, his other arm clutching the old man's waist. Easton wasn't much taller than Delby, thin, brown hair wild and uncombed.

"Please! Don't do this!" Delby pleaded, hands raised.

"Shut up, old man," said Easton, slow-walking him away from a table he'd been cleaning and toward the front counter. Easton mashed a silver pistol against the old man's cheek.

"Easton, you're lookin' at life if you kill him. Maybe even the death penalty. If you let him go, I can help you."

Slipping my Beretta out of its holster, I called in the hostage situation, asking for backup running silent. When dispatch acknowledged, I slid around the corner, sneaking toward the lunch counter.

Easton had his back to me, dragging Delby toward the door.

"I'm already lookin' at life," Easton snarled. "This old man's my shot at gettin' out of here."

"Easton!" I shouted, pistol extended. I held up my badge. "Detective Sinclair, seventh precinct. Lay down your weapon and put your hands behind your head. Now!"

Keeping the counter between me and Easton, I crept forward. Boone, on the other side of the counter, edged forward, both hands gripping his Glock.

"Stay back!" Easton shouted, voice quivering. "Or I'll splatter his brains all over the counter!"

A chill rolled over me. The standoff from my nightmares.

Delby's words played in my head as I kept my gun leveled at Easton, now caught between me and Boone.

When people's threads knot up like old fishing line, they come through the Monolith, the eye of the needle. For one chance to untangle or recast the line.

I had one shot at untangling this knot. If I failed, Delby—and maybe Boone—would die.

"You're making a big mistake," Delby said to Easton.

"Shut up, old man," Easton growled, gun muzzle tight against Delby's temple. He shifted his weight against the counter.

"Don't throw everything away like this," said Delby.

Easton slammed his pistol against the old man's head.

"I said shut the fuck up! God, you're worse than my cousin, Carl—never shuts up. At least he's useful. Got my shit back from your fucking evidence lockup." Easton laughed. "And some bonuses. Carl says stuff goes 'missing' all the time."

Carl Terry! The precinct clerk that managed access to the evidence lockup.

I slid closer until I'd run out of counter. Easton was about six feet from me now. Growing more and more agitated.

Backup wouldn't get here in time. This guy would blow at any moment, taking me, Boone, and Delby with him.

That's when the idea came to me. Maybe it'd only get me written up, not killed?

"Detective Boone's very familiar with the evidence lockup, aren't you, buddy? Word at the precinct is you shop there a lot."

"What?" Boone asked, confusion in his voice.

"You heard me," I said, poking my head up from behind the counter. "Whole precinct's talking about it. Said you paid for your upcoming vacation that way. Gonna hand out lots of marked bills as tips in Tahiti?"

"You think I stole evidence to pay for my cruise? Have you lost your mind, Chance? Easton, drop the weapon!"

I stepped around the counter, 9mm leveled at Boone's chest as I walked toward him.

Delby's face looked pale as I moved past. Easton pointed his gun at me, then back at Delby, looking confused as hell.

But no one looked more confused than Boone. His eyes were wide, pupils like black holes, watching me advance.

"Chance! What you doin'?" Boone shouted, southern accent thick, his face pale.

Mouth open, eyes wide, Boone stared at me, Glock still on Easton.

I stepped toward Boone again, heart hammering my chest, mouth going dry.

Boone backed away, boots clacking on old linoleum, skittering through trails of dirty moonlight that poured through the deli window.

"It's me – your partner!"

Boone thumped his chest, revolver jerking from Easton to me.

I leveled the barrel at his chest.

"Dirty cops deserve to die," I growled.

Easton was transfixed, watching the confrontation.

Boone's face was Formica-white as I slid my finger toward the trigger.

Turning, I put a shot into Easton's leg and lunged at him.

"Chance, no!" Boone shouted.

I grabbed Easton's gun as Boone pulled Delby backward.

The thunderous bang and flash of orange against smoke startled me.

Boone tackled Easton and cuffed him as I dropped to my knees, a dark stain spreading across my hoodie.

"The eye of the needle," I said.

Delby whispered in my ear. "You've just passed through it. But don't worry, I tied a knot at the end." He motioned to the floor.

Easton's hollow point lay on the dusty, checkered linoleum. I lifted my shirt, finding a deep graze.

"That co-jack cheese gave you temporary dispersion power," said Delby. Boone helped me up. "Bullet bounced right off."

"Sinclair!" Boone shouted. "Don't you ever pull a stunt like that again, you hear me?"

I just smiled.

"That whole interchange's goin' in my report, you got me?"

I nodded and hauled Easton to his feet.

Boone squeezed my shoulder. "Nice job," he whispered. "If you ever do it again, I'll kill you myself, kid. I'm not trainin' another partner, got it?"

"Had to wrap this up so Karen could have her anniversary cruise," I said as half the precinct rolled up to the Monolith's curb.

I came home to an empty bed and a note from Brit saying she needed a break. I forwarded her the accidental text and told her to come pick up her fucking couch.

I draped the decorative throw across the bed, hoping not to dream.

The next morning, Boone and I went back to the Monolith. A pretty redhead in a black apron was at the counter along with a grey-haired woman.

"Is Delby here?" I asked.

The redhead frowned, freckles scrunching across her pert little nose. "Delbert Higgins?"

I nodded.

"Not since 1939, when he passed away," said the grey-haired woman. "His daughter, Rose Higgins Sinclair, took it over but sold it in a few years. She had a peculiar son, as I recall. Raymond, I think."

I froze. "Raymond Sinclair?"

She nodded.

"That's...my father," I said, wide-eyed.

"Had horrible OCD?" the grey-haired woman asked.

I nodded.

"Used to order everything on the side and put his sandwiches together just so." Her voice fell to a whisper. "They say the boy was behind the counter during the robbery."

I frowned. "What robbery?"

The redhead's eyes widened. "Delby Higgins," said the grey-haired woman, "was shot and killed right behind this counter." She sighed.

"Over ten dollars and some change. His grandson saw the whole thing. Was never the same afterward."

The redhead gestured around the deli. "I always feel his presence, like he's still trying to help people. Gran says he used to say that the only way to get over a monolithic problem was to go through it."

"Through the eye of the needle," I said along with her.

"How'd you know that?" the redhead asked.

I smiled. "How do you know all this information?"

"Gran bought the deli from Rose Sinclair," she said. "And just sold it to me. That's why it was closed for renovations this week."

"Closed?" Boone cried, glancing at me.

"But I have Delby on the security camera footage."

The redhead shook her head. "There's no security camera here." She winked and slid me her business card. "My cell's on the back. When you're off duty, detective."

Boone slapped me on the back as we headed out of the deli.

"Enjoy that roast beef on Monday, kid."

"No, a cheeseburger."

"And break your routine?" Boone cried.

"For five years, I held myself to that routine, hoping if I kept everything the same, nothing bad would happen to my partner. My whole life, I've followed routines for that reason. Taking action keeps things safe."

"You ate roast beef every Monday for five years to keep me safe?"

I nodded.

Boone rubbed his eyes. "Let's get outta here, kid," he said, opening the door. "Someone's cuttin' onions."

I nodded and pulled off my St. Jude medallion, throwing it on a table. No more trying to control things. I'd see where life led me.

Maybe even make Delby—and my dad—proud.

Trafficking Stops

Sliver of moon was lost in the dark Illinois sky, truck stop's blinking signs polluting the cool June night as Sawyer Smith bought her first heroin balloon. From the truck stop's dark side where all the truckers parked for the night. Where anything—and anyone— under the moon and a blind eye could be bought, sold, or traded. And it was. Every. Single. Night.

Like the night her stepfather brought her here from Ohio and sold her to some monsters in Iowa. She had been fourteen.

Sawyer passed the rail thin man with wild eyes a twenty. He grabbed her arm, his hand grimy and pocked with track marks, fingernails caked with dirt. His breath reeked of alcohol, his body odor almost knocking her to the ground.

Sawyer froze, the memories of eleven years ago trickling back. The violence was as normal as the drinking and drugs and secrets she'd tried to keep. From the family that didn't want her. From the *boyfriends* and *brothers* offering her *help* as they passed her around like a broken thrift shop doll. From the lies she told herself, that all of this was normal, that she deserved it because she was worthless. And afraid. Until a night like this when she just—walked away. Bought a bus ticket to Pittsburgh and got off at the YWCA.

And told someone.

"How 'bout we do a trade, honey," he said, his gap-toothed leer unnerving.

She jerked free of his hold. "Not happenin'," she said with a growl and held out the twenty again.

He glared at her and yanked the bill out of her hand. "Fucking bitch."

And he was gone into the darkness and tangle of people working the night shift.

"You get all that, Radwell?"

Sawyer whispered into the night vision camera sewn into her blue hoodie, its lens pointing out of an eyelet where the drawstring used to be. The earpiece was tiny and fit into her ear. She wore torn-up skinny jeans, a ripped white V-neck T-shirt, and sneakers, looking more like seventeen than twenty-five with her short black hair high lighted blue to match her eyes. She slid the little red balloon deeper into her hoodie pocket.

Couldn't lose the evidence.

"That was too dangerous, Sawyer," said Corbyn Radwell in her ear, his voice deep and raspy, all business.

She didn't want a partner on this assignment, but her employer, Trafficking Stops, insisted. Hadn't five years of investigative work proven that she could handle any job thrown at her? Her evidence and information helped bring down dozens of human traffickers. Every conviction healed part of her pain. Every rescue cut away at the deep, cancerous fear that had always ruled her life. She loved her job.

She was a good spy.

"You got that, didn't you?" she said as she walked through the rows of parked trucks.

"Sure did," said the deep, raspy voice in her ear.

"Then get this. This isn't my first investigation, Radwell. I don't need a partner."

She'd lived this life. There were places like it all over the country. Where polite, trusting people followed their dreams and disappeared. Every. Single. Day. At fourteen, and the oldest of six siblings, she had left Gallipolis, Ohio (and horrible stepfather when her mother died) dreaming of being a singer. When she met her *boyfriend*. Who just wanted to help. Introduced her to heroin and meth. A dependent zombie, she was passed around to other ~~boyfriends and brothers~~ pimps. For four long years. Until she ended up as some bastard's sex toy in a tiny Nebraska town that tried to pretend she (and others like her) didn't exist. After she'd escaped.

We're all good people here, the mayor of that town told the media. *This kind of thing just doesn't happen.*

Too bad all the good people were out of town the night they sold her to a man and his son for four hundred bucks at the only gas and sip. They all turned a blind eye to her desperate looks and signals for help.

"Who's running your wireless hardware?" Radwell replied. "Backing up your information. And who's got your back if this all goes south? I do. And that's a promise."

She remembered him from Trafficking Stops' Seattle office and from running hardware on a few assignments. Tall and blond. Thirty something. Hazel eyes and cocky smile. All business in the field. He sounded sincere. For now.

Trust didn't come easily.

"So when's the big show?" she asked, changing the subject. "Take out your TracFone. Pretend you're on a call."

Sawyer pulled the phone out of her hoodie pocket and put it to her ear.

"Slaver's Shopping Club starts at eleven thirty; 'bout an hour away," said Radwell.

Sawyer winced, fear a sharp stab to her belly. She knew this place well. Sales of illegals and young teenagers (even kids) to the highest bidder held in the backs of rental trucks. She'd been sold twice here. No questions asked.

Nothing would make her happier than bringing this place down. "There's been a slight operation change."

"I don't like this, Radwell." She didn't like changes to the protocol they'd set up in the office.

"An informant came through with a seller's wristband. Remember, we talked about the possibility; but knew it was a long shot."

Sawyer chewed her lip. She vaguely remembered discussing it.

Having that route inside open up was a huge break in this case. She'd gladly walk into that monster pit if it brought them closer to closing it down.

"So, you and I are going in together. In the meantime, gather faces and evidence on camera. I've shared my location to your phone, but meet me at a green Mercury Cougar parked near the lot at 11:15 p.m. With Pearl Jam and Blind Melon stickers on the bumper. South side of the lot."

"No Nirvana or Weezer? You savage!" Sawyer said with a smirk. Radwell laughed. "My brother's the savage. It's his old car. Remember, Sawyer—no heroics. We're just taking pictures and gathering operations details. Getting one of these sales documented on camera. And then get out. Got it? Meet at the car. Hardware's in a truck labeled Midnight Sun Shipping with Alaska plates."

"How do I know you can pull this off?" Sawyer replied.

She knew nothing about Radwell and didn't like him giving all the orders. Why should she trust him?

His deep laugh echoed in her ear. "I've been a lot of things, Sawyer. Military. Police officer. Private security. Why should I trust you?"

"I lived this life for four horrible years until I escaped. Spent the last seven years learning to protect myself And I get a personal high from taking them out."

"Four years? Damn—that's rough."

"Seeya in an hour. How will I know it's you? It'll be dark and I can't risk standing out in this crowd. I need to ID you quick."

Radwell chuckled. "Look for the guy in the Nirvana T-shirt, black hoodie, and military haircut."

"That I've got to see," Sawyer said with a laugh. "Not sure I'll recognize you without your suit and tie."

No way Radwell had a Nirvana T-shirt. She put her TracFone back in her pocket and faded into the dark.

Sawyer walked through the dark lot that eclipsed the bright, dancing lights of the truck stop store and restaurant. The smell of cut grass and diesel fuel tanged the air, wind gritty from the surrounding farm fields. She moved through rows of dark trucks, capturing footage of rampant, small-time drug deals selling anything from crack to heroin. Everything was for sale. Or trade. There were more prostitutes than truck drivers.

She bought more drugs and eavesdropped on prostitution propositions, capturing details, hoping to find a lead up the chain and into its infrastructure. To the people running things. Most were hand to hands, supporting a family or a habit. Some were small-time brokers selling domestics and beats selling fakes or pushing shorts. She wanted the cartel marks and the slavers.

"You cheated me, you bastard!" shouted a man with brown dreads, shorts, and a Phish T-shirt at a man in baggy jeans, flip flops, and white T-shirt.

Sawyer stepped back as the fist fight started, capturing all of it on camera. The lot policed itself, so any fights or arguments were immediately squelched.

She moved away from the scene, heading south toward the lot's edge. To find Radwell.

She was early, but she found him leaning against the driver's side of the old green Cougar. She'd already checked the bumper from a distance and found the Pearl Jam and Blind Melon stickers.

She glanced at Radwell's wrist, seeing the white silicone bracelet. It had the word Admission printed in black. And sure enough, he wore a black Nirvana T-shirt, jeans, and black sneakers.

"How'd you do that?" Sawyer asked as she approached him.

She didn't remember him being so handsome with his rugged good looks, sexy tousled blond hair and sad hazel eyes, like a scolded puppy.

"What? The T-shirt?"

He tried to keep a straight face, but the smirk slipped through. "Okay, I traded it with the tech guy."

Sawyer couldn't help but laugh. He'd done that to impress her and dammit, it worked.

He moved beside her and leaned against her shoulder, whisper ing. "They've got security all along the perimeter, so we've gotta stay in char- acter. Got it."

Sawyer nodded.

"There are sales m four trucks tonight," Radwell whispered. "Each one has black bear in the name."

He grabbed her arm and pulled her against him. "Move, bitch or I'll drag you."

For a moment, Sawyer froze, the voices from her past taking hold, fear burning in the pit of her stomach as he led her through the darkness and the rows of trucks.

They walked down several rows of semis and large trucks until Black Bear Moving appeared at the end of a row. It was a huge semi trailer with two burly men standing in back.

The men glanced at Radwell's wrist. One of them stepped toward him, glaring, ignoring Sawyer. To him she was just cargo. Something to be sold and used. She wanted to rip the burly guy's head off.

"How about those Bears this year?" one of the men asked.

"How about those Cubs?" Radwell answered. "Best season ever."

The man glanced at Radwell's wrist and then turned and nodded at the other man who opened the trailer door, motioning Radwell inside.

Radwell grabbed Sawyer's arm again and pulled her up the ramp, toward the door.

"Resist," Radwell whispered.

Sawyer pulled away. "No! I'm not going in there!"

Radwell grabbed her arm and jerked her forward, allowing her to get the two men on camera. And the name on the truck.

"Shut your mouth or they'll find you in a ditch somewhere!" he said in such an angry voice that Sawyer recoiled from him.

Holding her against him, he pulled her forward. Inside the truck's dim-lit trailer.

Cigarette smoke hung in the air, giving the trailer an eerie fog-like presence as Radwell moved her through the crowd of men (and some women). The air smelled dry and stale with cigarette smoke and motor oil, voices a dull drone that reverberated against the metal walls. Ahead, at the front of the trailer, were three men with clip boards. And a group of ten women, each one with large black numbers hanging around their necks, eyes red, faces streaked with tears.

Sawyer heard muffled sobs as Radwell moved her closer.

And then she noticed men turning their eyes toward her, sizing her up like a 4-H calf up for auction. Her grip on Radwell's arm tightened, but she pushed back her fear, standing tall. Until Radwell hung a sign around her neck. With the number 1019.

She couldn't control her shaking as she watched them sell a long-legged redhead whose eyes looked far away on drugs. Or maybe she'd just withdrawn to keep her own sanity. Sawyer captured the sale on camera. And the next one, two fourteen-year-old girls sobbed and shook as they held onto each other.

The betting sky-rocketed, becoming a tinny roar that reverberated through the hollow trailer.

Two thousand. Three. Do I hear four grand?

At five grand they were sold to four muscled men in camo jackets.

"I can't do this, Radwell," she hissed in his ear. "Can't watch this."

Radwell held onto her arm. Made her look at him.

"Information first. Then the cavalry, okay?"

It took every ounce of strength she had to nod and stand there watching a fifteen-year-old girl screaming and crying as a man in a black shirt and jeans dragged her out of the trailer. Bought for a hundred bucks.

Sawyer felt sick. A hundred bucks. The price of a good set of head-phones. An e-reader. Small tablet. A fifteen-year-old meth addict. Things we don't think twice about when we shop.

This had to stop.

Sawyer moved away from Radwell, edging along the side of the trailer as the next bidding started. Where three young girls cowered against the metal wall. She slid down beside them. The first girl was short-haired like Sawyer, auburn hair and about fifteen.

"I'm so scared," she said to the girl beside her. Long brown hair and big brown eyes filled with tears.

"Why can't I just go home?"

Sawyer leaned toward them. "First chance you get, walk away. Walk into a store, a restaurant, a health club. Ask for help."

Both girls' eyes widened as they turned to stare at her.

"It just makes things worse," said the auburn-haired girl.

"Not if you don't go back to them," Sawyer replied. "Believe in yourself. You're not worthless. Fight for your life."

She leaned toward the middle girl, but the words froze on her tongue as she stared past her, at a young girl with black hair and blue eyes, a younger mirror of her own face. Her number was 999.

"Tabby?" Sawyer cried.

The young woman turned around, tears flooding her face. "Sawyer? Oh, my, God! Sawyer!"

Her little sister, Tabitha. Called Tabby. Sawyer threw her arms around her and held her tight.

Tabby was just eight when Sawyer left home. After Mom died and they were left with their horrible stepfather. Treated Mom's four kids like garbage. Sawyer hated him more than anyone in this world.

"How'd you get here?" Sawyer asked, brushing hair out of Tabby's face.

Tabby started to answer, but a stocky man grabbed hold of her and pulled her in front of the crowd.

"No! Tabby, no!"

Sawyer rushed back to Radwell.

"We have to do something," she said in his ear. "That's my little sister! Number 999."

Sawyer pointed at the young girl being paraded like a pony around the crowd. And there, standing on the side with a leering grin was her stepfather. In her head, he'd been tall and stocky. Fierce. Menacing with steely grey eyes, thick brown hair perfectly placed, and a heavy gait. But the monster had aged.

Seeing him now made her stomach churn, the old sour fear rising. But he looked grizzled, weathered, age hollowing his cheeks, brown eyes sunken into his face, still sharp and angry. Red and rheumy, nose and cheeks flushed. He lumbered with an uncertain shuffle, bald ing, unshaven, hands calloused and dirty, teeth missing from his leering grin, moving like an old alcoholic. Temper bubbling over, ready to explode. She'd seen it so many times.

"Get it on camera, Sawyer," Radwell said through gritted teeth.

"Buy her!" she shouted. "But I—"

Sawyer grabbed Radwell's arm and pushed his hand up.

"What are you doing?"

"Justice," she whispered.

Radwell grumbled, but kept bidding. Winning the bid at $500.

"Make sure you get footage of him taking the money," said Radwell.

Sawyer nodded, her heart pounding as she turned her camera toward Radwell as he walked up to that thin, balding monster with angry brown eyes and explosive temper. She captured all of it as Radwell pulled Tabby along beside him, heading back toward her. Tabby sobbed, hands against her face, but when she saw Sawyer, her sobbing softened. Radwell leaned down to her and said something she couldn't hear.

He grabbed Sawyer's arm, pulling her close. "We're leaving. Now."

Radwell lurched into the crowd, Tabby on one side, Sawyer on the other as they pushed their way toward the back of the trailer. Someone ahead knocked on the trailer door. It opened and then closed quickly.

When they'd gotten through the haze of smoke and press of bodies, Radwell pounded the door with his fist.

A heartbeat later, it opened. One of the burly men held up his arm, but Sawyer was ready for him.

She swung under his arm and ran down the ramp. The burly man chased after her. She heard other footfalls and then Radwell in her ear.

"Keep running! To the restaurant."

Sawyer ran as hard as her legs would pump, slipping behind trucks, through groups of people until the truck stop lights burned her eyes. Until she saw the Midnight Sun Shipping truck drive up beneath the sliver of moon. She ran toward the truck, climbing inside the tech van when the door slid open. The IT crew inside grinned at her.

"We got it all, Sawyer. All the evidence you need to take that guy down."

"I made sure to get every girl's face on film. And the—auctioneers. We'll start IDing everyone in the morning. I'll focus on rescuing the girls while I wait for the arrest warrants on their captors."

Sawyer collapsed into a chair and waited for Radwell and Tabby. It seemed like forever until the door opened and Radwell leaped inside, Tabby beside him. He slammed the door.

"Go! Now!"

The truck lurched forward and sped away onto the interstate. Only when they'd put a lot of distance between them and the truck stop did Sawyer relax. She reached over and patted her sister's hand.

"It's over now, kid."

Tabby nodded and threw her arms around her sister. "I thought you were dead. That's what he told us."

Radwell glanced over at Sawyer and grinned. "That footage is going to put him away for a long time."

"Thanks, Radwell," Sawyer said, returning his smile. "I know we broke protocol, but I couldn't walk out and leave Tabby like that."

"It's okay," he said in a quiet voice, nodding. "I'd have done the same thing."

<hr>

Eight months after the assignment, Sawyer flew from Seattle to Ohio for her stepfather's trial. It felt so good when the prosecutor played the evidence for the jury, showing her stepfather selling Tabby for $500. They took two hours to find him guilty.

A month later, Sawyer returned with Radwell and sat in the second row beside Tabby, listening as the judge sentenced that horrible man to life in prison. And Sawyer made sure that bastard looked into her eyes as they took him from the courtroom.

"Remember me, Eric?" Sawyer said.

Her stepfather glared at her. "I thought you were dead."

For the first time in her life, Sawyer saw that this man was only five foot nine at the most. The towering, explosive anger that had burned in his eyes had made them look so dark and menacing, but his brown eyes just looked cold. And empty. His shoulders sagged, a beer belly rounding over his brown pants. He looked like an old newspaper, yellowed and brittle, ink fading from the words so they had no meaning anymore. His soul was an ugly, sallow ashtray, crusty and stale with cigarette butts. Too cold to light even the memory of flame.

Sawyer stared through him, feeling like she towered over this grizzled monster.

"I'm sure you did," she snapped. "Too bad that the men you hired to sell me into—into hell sang like sparrows to the police. How ironic that selling Tabby is what sent you to prison?"

Sawyer turned away as they led her stepfather out of the court room, shouting and in cuffs. She moved over to Radwell. He put his arms around her and kissed her. They'd just moved in together after a few months of dating. She'd trust him with anything now.

"Nice work, Sawyer," he said.

Tabby hugged Sawyer and then Radwell. "Thank you both for everything."

"My pleasure," said Radwell.

The three of them walked out of the courthouse and out to a red Ford rental.

"Can't believe I'm going to live with you in Seattle," said Tabby, climbing into the back seat.

"Can't believe we're together," said Sawyer. "I'm still looking for Chris and Kayla."

She wouldn't turn a blind eye like the others. And she wouldn't stop searching until all four of them were together. Sawyer glanced at Radwell as he started the car. With Radwell as her partner, she could succeed at damn near anything.

Wild Nights and New Roads

So I have these episodes, right? I call them flares, like a blinding flashbulb going off in my face. Everything starts to move slow —like strobe-light slow—and the whole scene rolls in front of me.

Someone dying. Murder, accident, suicide, you name it. I see who's doing it and who's dying, but not when or where.

And just like that, the images are gone. And it's not like I can pause or rewind them either.

I never know when I'm going to get one or how it's gonna hit me either.

Sometimes, a handshake, sometimes just standing near the victim. I always try to warn them, but with almost no information, how do I just blurt that out to a stranger? I'm just a random guy with some vague random warning.

Hi, know we just met and all, but you're gonna be robbed and murdered soon by a man giving away a coffee table. He's balding with brown hair, wearing glasses, and a Bears T-shirt. I'm totally not hitting on you, lady. What? Fuck off or you'll call the cops. Right, just leaving.

It *kills* me to see this shit online in a few days. Knowing that the whole sordid thing played out just like I saw it. But I couldn't stop it.

This flare's different this time.

Over the past few days, I've had several of these flares stop me cold. So many—ten, twelve, fifteen—all at the same place. A place I recognize. And there was a sign. An actual sign that read, *Starlight*. It's a new club in Portland's Pearl District, lots of younger people go there. Inclusive, that sort of thing. Oh, and the date on the sign: *Christmas Eve*.

Christmas Eve was just a day away and the flares have been piling up. This time, it's gonna be different. This time, I'm going to stop it. Can't live with myself if something terrible happens there with me knowing when and where. That's half the battle!

Starlight is all glass and purple lights, its dark ceiling twinkling with stars like a regular galaxy or something. Christmas trees are all over the room in different colors and twinkling lights, swaths of fresh greenery lining the frosted glass walls. Big booths line three walls and a bar stretches across the fourth wall. Through a large archway adjacent to the bar, lights flash, colors changing.

The dance floor.

Its distant beat thrums through my body as I sit down in a white leather booth, the glass table showing my crummy hiking boots and jeans. Smell of fresh pine hangs above a cloud of colognes and after-shaves. Christmas carols fill the dining room, Bing bringing it home with *White Christmas*.

Can't believe how many people are here tonight, but hey, not every-body has a warm hearth and family sitting around a present-stuffed Christmas tree. A lot of us spend that night alone binging on Netflix, feeling worthless with a frozen dinner and some booze to cut the loneliness.

And memories of when we had all that and more.

My ex-wife Jessica would have loved this place. She moved to Cali-fornia to find a new life, with me not in it, of course. I can't blame her. Not sure anyone could live with this *gift* of mine (myself included). And Christmas was always the worst. We'd go to a friend's party or to her parents' place on the coast. I'd spend half the time in the bathroom getting blind-ass drunk, reeling from the flares crackling like popcorn. Knowing that my wife's niece was going to have a car accident on the way home or seeing the stroke her dad was about to have.

It was too much. Especially when Jessica refused to listen at all.

To them, I must have looked like a lunatic or an alcoholic. Ha! Jokes on them. I'm a lunatic AND an alcoholic. Coping mechanisms. This damned *gift* of mine's killing me. Don't know why I have it because most of the time, I can't help anyone. It's been useless torture.

But tonight—yeah, Christmas Eve—something bad, something real bad's going down at this club. And this time, I'm gonna be here to stop it. I brought my Glock in its shoulder holster and a spare clipped to my right side, tan canvas coat covering both. I have a concealed carry license. Former cop. Long story, but I left on good terms.

The overload of flares in that job was just too much for me.

A waiter in black pants, red Santa hat, and sleeveless white tuxedo shirt comes to my table. He plops down a coaster, tells me the drink and food specials, and takes my order. Cheeseburger and a top shelf, double scotch—neat. Don't want anything dulling my meds.

In a minute, he returns with my scotch, setting it down in a square glass dotted with glow-in-the-dark stars. The clink of glasses and ice is steady behind me from the bar. The waiter's hand brushes against mine.

Flashbulb sparks. Light strobes. Everything oozes slowly forward.

I suck in a breath when I see him. The gun man. In jeans and flannel shirt. Firing a hand gun. The whole room explodes in chaos. Face after face rushes past me. People up front by the door. On the dance floor. In the booths. More red than a Macy's Christmas parade. This waiter's gonna be shot and killed here tonight. Like the Pulse nightclub all over again.

I snatch up the scotch as the images quiet. The waiter's already gone. I slam the shot until it burns my gut, hoping it will stop my shaking.

But one last flare pulses across my eyes. Stops me cold, my heart pounding against my rib cage like a jackhammer.

My own face stares back at me. I'm on the floor. Bleeding out.

Stunned, I clench the empty shot glass in my fist. So, I've managed to change the outcome. Dead isn't what I wanted, but just the fact that something changed with me trying to stop it gives me hope. Hell, maybe I can even change the weather forecast, make a little Christmas Eve snow happen. Of course, Portland would come to a complete stop, abandon its cars, and close roads. Better not.

I look around. Lots of guys in flannel shirts and jeans.

The waiter returns with my cheeseburger. I ask him for another shot. As he sets down the mustard and ketchup, I notice a woman in a curve-hugging red dress staring at me over a glass of red wine. Her red hair is bone-straight around her oval face, framing a bright smile and big, electric green eyes. Her fingernails are as glossy red as a candy apple red Mustang on Christmas Day. The light glints off them in little star-like pinpoints of purple light.

She's staring at me.

I look around, expecting some dude in a tux to walk up behind me and wave at her, but no one's there. Not sure why, but she's staring at me.

I put some ketchup and mustard on my cheeseburger and dig into it as *Jingle Bell Rock* ripples through the room, brightening the mood. If Bing starts warbling *I'll Be Home for Christmas*, I swear I'll slit my wrists with this shot glass.

When I finish my cheeseburger, I set the plate aside and wipe my mouth with the white cloth napkin, feeling guilty about getting ketchup and mustard on it. I pick up my scotch.

As I look across the room, the woman is gone.

I throw back my scotch and rest my elbows on the table. That's when I feel someone next to me. I turn.

The lady in the hottest Christmas red dress I'd ever seen.

"Hey there, handsome," she says to me and I almost laugh.

She wants to sell me something.

"Hello, lovely lady," I reply. I can play this game, too.

"Mind if I sit down? It looks like I've been stood up."

"Be my guest."

Always ready to help, including a woman that can obviously take care of herself and then some. I motion toward the other side of the booth and she slides across the white leather, glass of red wine in her fist. And yes, she's absolutely beautiful close-up, too. I don't want to lose my focus on the room, so I try to ignore her a little. But damn, it's hard with those haunting green eyes. And those long legs beneath the glass table.

"I'm Emma," she says.

I nod. "Dan. Nice to meet you, Emma."

So, the dance begins.

"What do you do?" she asks. "You look like a surfer with all that blond hair and lean build."

I think she just winked at me. I let her flattery go.

"I'm a substance abuse counselor," I tell her. I know all the best ways to abuse substances and still be functional, believe me. "Wish I could say it was in Malibu, but I'm a local. What do you do, Emma? Modeling? Acting? Just passing through Portland?"

She nods. "On my way south tomorrow."

"To Christmas Day with family?" I ask.

"Something like that," she answers, those damned green eyes so hypnotic.

Glass shatters behind me and I jump, my heart racing.

"Relax," she says with a smile. "Bartender just dropped some glasses."

I nod as she stares at me, like she could look past my eyes into my skull and read every thought I've ever had. Like she somehow knows about my *gift*. Like she can almost see it.

"You seem awfully nervous," she says in a quiet voice as she reaches across the table and lays her hot hand on top of mine.

I've never felt such a warm hand in my entire life. But the moment her hand touches mine, images strobe through my brain. Faces, bodies, people screaming, and so much blood.

"It doesn't have to be this way," she says in a half-whisper as the flare loops and loops.

I pull away from her, but she grabs my hand and holds it tight in her fist.

"Do you hear me, Dan? We can stop it."

"Stop what?" I snap, jerking my hand out of her grasp. How does she know what I'm seeing?

"Listen, I know I must sound crazy to you, but I have this weird ability, sort of like premonitions. I came here to stop this."

I laugh, squeezing my eyes closed. "Me too. See, I have the same weird ability. I see people's fates and so many will die tonight if I can't stop it." I start to shake all over. "Tell me, what do you see?"

"I see through the gun man's eyes. So I know everything he's going to do and where, but that's all."

"Wait, so you can see through the gun man's eyes? That's wonderful! I see the rest of it. How it unfolds. Who dies. Maybe together—"

A shot rings out.

Someone screams. It was starting to happen.

I jump up from the booth, cop instincts kicking in high gear.

"Dan, wait!" She shouts, struggling out of the booth.

But I'm already running toward the sound. Ahead, I see my waiter, standing over a table. They're shrieking, a spray of red all over the white leather seats and the glass tabletop. He's holding the weapon in his hand.

I draw my Glock, shouting for him to drop it.

He just stares at me, swiveling around, the weapon glinting silver in his hand.

The heat of her hand is a wildfire against my neck.

A flare strobes across my eyes, but it's not my own. Somehow, she's passing her vision to me.

As my finger touches the trigger, I see myself through her eyes. Killing the waiter. And seven people at the table. Two more on the dance floor. Until the razor-sharp burn of bullets thump into my chest. From a gun-carrying Good Samaritan. Catching bystanders in the crossfire.

Blood stains my flannel shirt and jeans as I collapse onto the dance floor, the bass still throbbing through my chest as I gurgle, bleeding from everywhere.

Then I see the waiter's blood-stained hand. And the weapon—a silver wine opener. Not a hand gun. The pop was a bottle of champagne. And they'd broken a bottle of red wine.

My God. It's me. I'm the killer.

I can't move, the horror flooding over me.

Emma's hand presses against mine holding the gun and the heat of her skin makes my hand relax. Slowly, she takes the gun from my hand as I drop to my knees, shaking.

She puts a hand over my eyes and everything turns black a moment.

When it clears, I'm back sitting at the booth, Emma holding onto my hand.

"You didn't let me finish, Dan," she says as my other hand flies to my chest, searching for all the bullet entry wounds.

But there aren't any.

"What just happened?" I blurt out. "I was bleeding out on that dance floor!"

"Part of my gift lets you experience what you're about to do, see what the result of your actions are—that kind of thing. You just lived through the blood bath you've been seeing in your head for days. And I just showed you how it happens and how it ends."

The loud pop, like a gunshot rings out. Shrieks cut through the Christmas carols.

My entire body flinches, cop reflexes fighting to surface, to act, but I concentrate on Emma's hand, forcing myself to stay seated.

The minutes tick by. No other *pop-pop* sounds ring out. No more screams.

Soon, the din of dishes and conversations are a dull buzz through the room, punctuated with laughter, *Holly Jolly Christmas,* and the bass thrum of distant dance music fill the lull.

I look across the table. Emma's smiling at me now.

"I've seen your face in my head for days," she says. "Your long struggle with PTSD. I've felt what you've felt, so I know you were here to stop this, too." She smiles at me. "I also saw something else."

"What'd you see?" I ask, eyes widening, concerned again.

"Here, let me show you."

She slides out of the booth and pushes me over. She slides in beside me now. With those long red nails, she presses her hand over my eyes. The burn is sharp. She's showing me something through my own eyes. The two of us—together.

I'm grinning.

She slides another scotch over to me and lifts her glass of red wine.

"A toast," she says, still smiling. "To wild nights and new roads."

That's the best damned offer I've ever had.

"Merry Christmas, Emma." I say, clinking her glass with mine and then sipping my scotch.

She reaches over and pushes a lock of blond hair out of my eyes. "Merry Christmas, Dan."

"So what should we call this new partnership?" I ask. "Now, that we're apparently going into business together as private detectives."

She leans over and kisses me on the lips. "With both our gifts, we'll be great together. But I can't see that far ahead."

"Good," I reply.

Because I don't want to skip to the end and ruin a happy ending.

I pull her into a proper kiss. Relieved that sparks, not flares, flood my body as Bing winds up with *Silver Bells*.

Permanent Ink

THE AUTOCLAVE SPUTTERED THROUGH THE WELL-LIT tattoo studio, momentarily drowning out the steady hum of needles and ink against flesh, as it cleansed equipment. Persephone slouched against the wall and peered out the picture window as she waited for her next client. The Bainbridge ferry glided across Elliot Bay's gunmetal surface, stark white against another grey on grey day in Seattle. August was slipping into September. She would have to leave soon.

Scowling, she laid her hand against the yellowing flash sheets pasted on the studio wall, her fingers tracing brightly colored tribal symbols, yin yangs, and Celtic knotwork set against the tropical orange paint. Soulless designs with little understanding of the cultures they depicted. She crossed her arms. Only the gods knew how lost these languages were to mortals whose feet passed so quickly across this earth. How different the world seemed these thousand years or so, but for her, so little had changed.

"Coffee, Seph?"

She glanced at the styrofoam cup of instant coffee and powdered creamer that Nick Malone held out to her. Everything designed to be disposable. With a hundred coffee vendors in this town selling fresh roast, Nick was drinking instant. She barely smelled the coffee above the studio's antiseptic tinge. But she couldn't fault the man. He was over-worked and much too busy to run down the street for fresh coffee. The impatience of mortals was tiring. Behind her, the autoclave hissed its warm breath through the room. She found its rhythmic sounds comforting and she liked making an effort to cleanse and reuse the old.

"No, thank you," she answered with a brief smile, her voice low and sleepy. "I can't drink that powdered swill."

Nick owned the studio and let her work for him every summer. His chestnut hair was long and tied in a ponytail at his nape. One of his ears was pierced four times with silver studs. He wore a yellow T-shirt and both of his lanky, upper arms were sleeved in intricate tribal symbols drawn in bold primary colors. He was wiry and tall, his green eyes bright. He stood beside her and sipped from the cup. She'd known Nick almost ten years now. Despite his mortal flaws, he was wise and she trusted him.

"You'll be leaving soon, won't you?"

She turned around and stared at him for a moment. "But I never said a word about—"

"You didn't have to," he said and nodded toward the window. "I always know. Every year, just before you stop showing up, you spend a lot of time in front of this window. Like you're gathering a picture to take with you." He smiled. "When I see those leaves fall, I always know you won't be back until spring."

He pointed toward the row of green trees outside the shop. They hadn't started to turn yet. And as long as she remained here, they would be green. Of the mortals she knew, Nick was sometimes more observant than she realized.

"Look, Seph," he said, staring into the cup, "I've never asked you where you go or anything about your personal life. It's none of my busi-ness. You've seemed so troubled this year—so I just wanted to give you a little advice."

"I'm listening."

His index finger slid around the cup's rim. "I don't know why you have to leave every summer, but I just think you'd be happier if you made a choice between Seattle and wherever else, that's all."

She knew he was right, but she didn't have the luxury of such a choice. She was caught between two worlds. A world of winter and death for half the year and a world of sunlight and transition for the other half. For centuries she'd stoically endured this half-life, but now—she couldn't bear to return to the underworld.

Nick nudged the tropical orange wall with the toe of his grungy loafers. "You're one of the best tattooists I've ever had work for me. Ever. The original artwork you create is straight out of legend. So real... sometimes, it's frightening."

She bowed her head and sighed. If only she could tell him everything. If only she could show him what she'd seen through the ages. Civilizations rise then fall, languages flow then ebb, symbols etched then faded. She was there when Babylon fell to Persia, when the Celts rose to power, and when the Romans conquered Greece. She had walked alongside Aristotle and attended Sophocles' first play. But she'd never watched the leaves turn or the snow fall. She'd never seen all the seasons pass before her eyes.

"Dump the guy, Seph," he said with a wry smile. "It's not worth it, if you aren't happy."

Persephone's smile faded as she turned toward the window. Mortals had such narrow focuses, but the more she thought about Nick's words, the truer they rang. And the question she'd been too afraid to utter rolled over her tongue.

Leave Hades?

She'd eaten the food of the dead—six pomegranate seeds—and those seeds forever bound her to the underworld and her lover, Hades. She laid her hand to her stomach where she'd had six of the glistening red seeds tattooed. Ironic that such a permanent mark signified her transient life.

"I wish it were that simple."

The Nereids had warned her about Hades—all stern and darkness. Dull and lifeless, Hecate had lamented. But from the first moment she'd seen him in that great onyx chariot, she knew a gentle, passionate, and misunderstood man lay beneath his stern exterior. It hadn't been his choice, but he'd dutifully donned the underworld's facade. It was expected of him. But since she'd been with him, his hair had lightened to a sandy brown with hints of sunlight at her touch and his eyes had softened to a kind brown. For her, he'd gathered the shiniest gemstones and the most precious metals, lighting the dark confines of his castle with as much brilliance as the underworld could manifest. Without her touch, she knew his castle would quickly go dark again.

She sighed. And so would he. How could she doom him to that life now when he had finally tasted sunlight? Even if it was only part of a year?

As he had held the sunlight in his palm, so had she felt the stillness and shadows touch her soul. It would hurt him terribly, but she could not endure another winter below ground. She needed to belong somewhere and if that meant challenging the gods' curse, then she would challenge it.

Nick squeezed her shoulder. "Then simplify it," he said and turned away.

His heavy footsteps clomped across the wooden floor.

"Seph, your two o'clock is here," called Nancy from the appointment desk.

Persephone swept her dark hair off her shoulder and moved toward her station. An antique green barber's chair framed by a black, L-shaped table containing her inks, needles, and supplies. A small rolling stool was pushed underneath one of her tables. She checked the needles she had soldered and sterilized. Everything was ready. Satisfied, she went over to greet her client.

A blond young man wearing baggy, faded jeans and a short-sleeved shirt stood beside the counter. Beside him, a dark-haired young woman in cargo shorts and a red T-shirt clung to his arm.

"So you decided to do it?" said Persephone. She had talked to the couple last week about designs and the process.

The young woman nodded. "I'm a little nervous," she said and giggled. She scrunched her face. "Will it hurt?"

Persephone laughed. "Of course, it will hurt. They're needles, remember?"

"You'll be fine, Trace," said the young man, nudging her with his shoulder.

Persephone motioned them to follow as she moved back to her station.

"Okay," said the woman, shuffling her Birkenstocks across the shiny tile floor. "If I hate it, I can always have it removed."

Persephone halted in mid-stride and turned. "You're not ready for a tattoo."

Startled, the young woman stared at her. "Sure I am!"

"No, you're only half certain that you want it," she replied, shaking her head.

She led them over to Craig's station against the far wall. In his chair, lay a man having a tiger's head tattooed on his chest. Craig, a thin young man with close-cropped blond-tipped dark hair, was hunched over the man. He wiped away spots of blood and excess ink with a sterile pad while he applied a fine blush of orange pigment with the tattoo machine. The machine's steady buzzing and the grimace on the man's face made the young woman grow pale.

Persephone pointed at the outline of the tiger's face. "A tattoo isn't a decal you can peel off and on. It's a something you're committing to, a permanent choice."

She pointed to the Celtic knotwork she'd tattooed on Craig's wrist. The intricate twining of granite lines and rich symbols had been drawn centuries ago by a young warrior who dreamed of the sea. In those lines, was a story of that warrior's first sea voyage and she had passed on that story when she'd reproduced it on Craig's arm. What began as a young man's journey became a symbol of courage to Craig.

"Go home and think about it," she said, laying her hand on the young woman's shoulder. "And ask yourself some hard questions. Who are you? What do you aspire to be? What symbolizes your life? When you know, you'll be ready for this tattoo."

The young woman stared at her for a few moments then stole a quick glance at the man gripping the chair arms. "You're right. Thank you." She nodded at her boyfriend. "Let's go, Andre."

For a moment, all Persephone heard was the whisper of the Aegean Sea in the autoclave's hiss. But it was all one ocean. She needed to ask herself those very same questions.

"That was nice, Seph," said Nick. He was standing beside her now. "Not everyone would have done that."

She gazed at him with the mixture of Eleusian and Babylonian images encircling his upper arms. By marking himself with these ancient teachings and prayers, he'd committed himself to those ways. She moved in front of the full-length mirror on the post beside Craig's station and studied herself.

Except for the pomegranate seeds on her stomach, there were no other tattoos on her skin. Not one. She held up her hands. No rings either. Nothing to symbolize her union with Hades. Nothing to represent conviction of any kind. Just the seeds of the gods' curse. And because of that curse, she'd been treating her own life like an old coat, something to drag out only when she felt cold.

Who was she? She didn't know anymore.

"But what I said is true, Nick." She turned toward him. "It's not a haircut that grows out or a shirt you take off and wash." Or a place she stayed for only half the year. "Either you get one or you don't. There's no in-between."

She knew what she had to do.

Turning in her sandals, Persephone hurried to her station and grabbed her purse.

"Nancy, cancel all my appointments for the week," she called to the curly-haired receptionist.

Nick frowned. "You're leaving?"

She nodded, but let a smile curve across her face. "But this time, I'll be back."

She rushed past the autoclave in the back room and slipped outside into the flurry of downtown Seattle. A quick bus ride would get her to the ferry. Only between land and sea where it was all one ocean, could she summon the crossroads to the underworld.

One last time, she would stand at the edge of the underworld's domain to bid her lover farewell. One last time.

THE AIR WAS COOL AGAINST HER FACE AS SHE STOOD ON THE ferry's bow, waiting for it to slip gently across the bay. She'd taken this journey so many times over the years. On boats, ships, yachts, and triremes. In every body of water in the world. But this would be her last.

After the ferry's mournful call, it slowly slipped into the bay. Seattle's skyline slid into the distance, fading into the ubiquitous grey haze over Seattle. The emerald city glittered like a smoky jewel. Persephone was eager to watch the leaves turn red and gold and fall to the earth.

She turned her gaze to Elliott bay. Two porpoises leaped in front of the ferry's bow. Smiling, she leaned against the railing, watching the sleek black and white porpoises. Beside them, Nereids played. She watched their glittering seafoam bodies surge through the wake beside the porpoises. They giggled and chattered at her.

"Persephone! We've missed you!" they called in child-like voices. "Come and play with us."

Whenever she'd made this journey before, the Nereids' presence had always made her sad. Now, they made her laugh.

"Next trip," she whispered into the wind.

The wind swirled past the Nereids, carrying her words to them.

"Do you promise?" one of them asked, her seaweed hair flowing around her cherubic face and slender shoulders.

Persephone nodded. She looked forward to it.

Waving, the Nereids plunged beneath the surface and sped away with the porpoises.

Persephone turned her face into the wind. "My dear friend, Hecate, I call for the crossroads." Taking a deep breath, she reached out her hands to the air.

Shadowy hands reached out and grasped her hands, pulling her from the ferry's deck.

There was a rush of shadows and then she stood in the middle of a crossroad. Three footpaths, worn smooth, ambled into a tangle of trees and brush. Woods surrounded her on all sides, cedar trees towering above the ruddy trunks of madrone trees. The air smelled of sea salt and fresh rain.

"Hecate!" she called, turning to look in all directions.

She waited, but no one answered.

"Hecate, please!"

At last, Hecate appeared on the center path and walked toward her. Her eyes were the color of ebony. She wore a long, thin dress of shimmery charcoal that clung to her slim body.

"Persephone," she said, her voice low and gravely. "You're early this season. Hades will be so pleased. You should see the improvements he has made to the castle in your absence." She turned and started down the path that led toward a shadow looming ahead.

Persephone sighed, following with reticent steps. This would hurt him deeply. She had no wish to hurt him, but pleasing him was destroying her.

"I'll follow you to the gates, but no farther. Please ask Hades to meet me there."

"What? But why the gates?" she turned and scrutinized Persephone. "Has something happened?"

Yes, she had finally grown up. She wasn't that foolish little girl picking flowers near Eleusis or the headstrong young woman trying to ignore her mistakes and their consequences. She was the daughter of a goddess. Even if the gods took her god-essence, she would break this curse.

"Please ask him to come to me."

Hecate's thin face shadowed with concern as she turned away, rushing ahead and fading into the shadows. With slow steps, Persephone followed until she felt the shadow engulf her.

For a moment, she was falling. She closed her eyes until the ground felt solid against her sandals again. A long corridor stretched ahead toward dim light and shadows. The air smelled cold and stale—gritty. She shivered, feeling the cold of shades as they passed around her, heading toward the gates. They had already crossed over on Charon's ferry and would spend the rest of their days here until they were allowed to cross over to the Elysian Fields.

And into the sunlight, Persephone thought with a sigh and folded her arms against her torso.

Ahead, the massive black gate rose, casting a long, dark shadow on the path. Cerberus crouched beside the gate, a low growl crackling in the silence. She moved toward the massive, three-headed dog.

"Cerberus?"

When the three-headed dog saw her, his serpent tail thumped against the ground. He whimpered and scrambled toward her. His three canine tongues licked her hands and feet as he pranced around her. Smiling, she knelt beside him and stroked one of his napes.

"He's missed you."

She froze at the sound of Hades' velvet voice.

Inhaling slowly, she rose from the ground, afraid to look into his eyes. He lifted her chin. A smile lit his pale complexion, his brown eyes bright.

"Have you at last missed me? Is that why you've returned home so soon?" His strong hands cupped her face, warming against her skin.

She slipped away from his touch and the smile fled from his face.

"No," she answered, looking away. "I've come to tell you that—" She sighed. "This is difficult."

His hands were at her shoulders and she felt his kiss against her neck.

"What is it, my love?" he asked, his voice soft and distracted.

She turned, holding him at arm's length. "I've come to tell you that —I won't be coming back here."

He laughed for a moment, but his voice quickly faded, the shock at last dulling his features.

"You're serious, aren't you?"

She nodded. "I am so weary of living two lives, Hades." She bit her lip and slid her hand into his. Gently, she brought his hand to her face and pressed his fingers to her lips, kissing them. "My soul is dying in this empty place. You have been the only brightness in this realm, but that isn't enough anymore."

"What of the curse?" he said in a half-whisper.

"I—I don't know what will happen, but if it will end this constant migration, I will risk it."

Sadness touched his face, his brown eyes growing watery as he pulled his hand away. "Do I still mean nothing to you? After all this time?"

She closed her eyes. He meant so much to her, but it wasn't enough. He only loved her under his terms. She had sacrificed everything for him, yet his love only lasted six months of the year. She felt like a wild-flower, brittle from frost, dying slowly with the sun's rise.

"I ask the same of you, Hades. I don't think you've ever known me at all."

Anger sharpened his features. "You'll return," he snapped. "You won't risk your immortal soul—not for this." He cast a hurt, longing gaze at her and then turned away, trudging toward the gates. Already, his form was greying in the dim light.

She waited until he disappeared into the shadows before she turned and walked away from the gates, back toward the crossroads. As she stepped through, everything darkened until she felt the deck of the Bainbridge Island ferry beneath her. It was evening and the city glittered against the dark waters. She huddled against the railing, the air chilly, and watched the lights until the ferry reached the dock.

What would happen to her when she failed to return to the underworld? What price would she pay for swallowing six pomegranate seeds?

SEPTEMBER WANED AND THE LEAVES DID NOT TURN. Already, Persephone felt the pull that had already begun to tug at her limbs. Autumn had not arrived. Everyone talked about the oddness of the season, but the mortals moved ahead with their lives.

Persephone stood near one of the flower stands at Pike's Market, admiring the bunches of wildflowers wrapped in slick green paper. Standing in front of so many flowers reminded her of distant childhood, before she had encountered Hades. How far away that life seemed now. The damp air was fresh with vegetable and flower scents, the fish smell only a distant tinge from the nearby fish market.

In her ears, Hecate's husky whisper called her back to the underworld. Persephone hummed, trying to drown out the scratchy call in her ears. Over the next few days, that whisper would quickly grow shrill and piercing.

But she would not yield. Not this time.

She bought herself a bouquet of purple and yellow flowers and walked away from the crowd.

Below, at street level, Persephone watched the cars slip past the piers. She hurried down the sprawling flights of stairs and across the street until she'd reached the pier. Beyond the shops and the aquarium to the misty bay waters.

She sighed. How long would Hades wait for her at the underworld gates? How long would it take before he realized she wasn't coming back?

AS MORNING SLIPPED INTO AFTERNOON, THE SKY DARKENED. The bay grew choppy as the wind howled across the piers. Persephone folded her arms against her stomach, the chilly wind cutting through her, and tried to make her way to the bus stop.

In an instant, the world froze around her, standing motionless. Everything halted and there was only silence. Even the bay turned mirror-calm.

The sound of a great door creaking open filled the silence. Persephone trembled. She had only heard that sound once in her life, but she had never forgotten it.

It was the sound of Fate.

She laid her hand to her quivering stomach. Even the gods had masters and Fate was one of those forces. It had come to exact the curse on her.

Raindrops hit the pavement. She looked closer, reaching out to touch them—red splotches—and pulled her hand away. Droplets of blood wept from her palm where those awful pomegranate seeds had first rested.

"You defy your immortality, Persephone," said a rough voice.

The sound floated around her.

"I want my freedom!" she shouted, turning around. The blood stained her shirt and droplets continued to fall against the pavement. "I cannot keep wandering between lives."

Abruptly, a ring of smoke undulated around her head then swirled away, coalescing into a stone-faced figure in front of her. The hazy presence looked neither male nor female.

"Then you have made your choice."

A smoky hand moved toward her and plunged into her chest.

She gasped, her knees buckling.

As the hand plucked the gleaming sphere of ambrosial god essence from her chest, she collapsed against the blood-spattered pavement.

The air rustled with yellow and red leaves that clattered against the sidewalk. She turned to look at the trees. They were dying! All their radiant yellow leaves were blowing away, leaving behind skeletal trunks and limbs. The winter snows would blow soon and everything would sleep until spring.

She began to tremble. There was no difference between this place and the underworld. Her stomach clenched.

What had she done?

Immediately, the roar of Seattle crescendoed around her. Cars honking, people jogging, voices chattering. She huddled against the sidewalk, unable to gather the strength to rise to her feet. People walked around her as if she no longer existed.

"Someone, please—help me," she called.

No one answered.

Feeling frightened and lost, she huddled there for a long time until at last, a hand touched her shoulder.

"Let me help you," said a velvety, soft voice.

She looked up, relieved that someone had heard her.

Those kind brown eyes, the light brown hair. Hades! Here, among the living?

"Why are you here?"

He wore simple black trousers and a white shirt, looking humble and sweet. Smiling, he laid his fingers against her lips.

"It doesn't matter anymore. I knew that Fate would tear the god essence from your soul if you did not heed the curse." Tenderly, he brushed the hair out of her eyes and held out his other hand to her. A gleaming sphere the color of citrine lay in his palm. "I've brought you ambrosia."

Her eyes grew teary. "Why would you restore me—after I left you?"

His eyes turned sad. "I would rather have you gone from me than gone from the world." He stroked her black hair. "The curse is broken now. At least this way, I can still gaze on you from time to time."

Hades pressed the ambrosia to her lips. The sphere dissolved into sweet nectar that slid down her throat and warmed her belly. She held onto his arms and struggled to stand.

"You'll be weak for a few days, but then you will feel yourself again."

With a sigh, he kissed her on the forehead and turned toward the ferry dock.

"Hades," she called.

He stopped, but did not turn.

"My whole life, since I've been with you," said Persephone, "I've always lived on your terms. You loved me as long as I remained below with you. When I was gone from you, was it me or the sunlight that you missed?"

Hades turned, no expression on his face. "My life was planned out for me, Persephone, guiding the dead on their journey. My days are filled with their confusion and senselessness. When I saw you that day picking flowers in the field, glowing with beauty and peace—I was overcome. I want that in my life even if it's only for half the year."

His gaze fell to the sidewalk.

"Was I selfish? Of course. But you are finally free of me. I cannot hold you now."

Persephone sighed. "How I wished that one time over the centuries, you'd have asked to come with me. To share my world as I shared yours."

"I never knew how much you cherished your mortal existence." He looked up, sadness in his eyes. "I never thought past meeting you at the gate."

"Are you so blind that you don't see that I grew to love you?" Persephone asked, walking slowly toward him. "It held me more than those six pomegranate seeds ever did. All I've ever wanted to hear was your voice calling me back because you loved me."

He sighed and closed his eyes. "Come home, Persephone. I'm only a shade without you."

"Maybe there is a way that I can come home to you?"

His watery eyes snapped open. "Tell me! If there is something that will keep you in my life, I will gladly do it."

"Raise your castle," she replied. "Allow it to reside both in the underworld and in this world, so I can look on this place while nature slumbers. And sometimes—in spring or summer—walk with me in this world."

Hades thought for a moment, turning to stare at Elliott Bay. "What would Zeus say?"

"Does it matter?" Persephone asked. "You are lord of the under-world. What do *you* say?"

A faint smile lit his pale face for a moment. "I say that without you, I'm dead inside."

At last, he moved toward her and took her in his arms. His kiss was long and deep, gentle as falling snow, but Persephone felt his passion, his urgency. She melted into his touch.

"With Poseidon's help," Hades whispered, "I'll raise my castle—if you'll stay with me."

She nodded and lifted her shirt, revealing the six pomegranate seeds tattooed across her stomach like little ruby teardrops. At last, they meant something permanent to her.

"The pomegranate seeds are forever," said Persephone, her coal black hair against her cheek.

Tenderly, he ran his fingers across the little teardrops. "Why, Persephone? The curse has been lifted."

"Because I love you."

Moved by the symbol, he could not speak for a moment, his eyes brimming with moisture.

Finally, he took her hand in his. "In the spring, show me your world," he said in a soft voice. "But please—come home now."

"Why?" Persephone asked.

"Because I love you," he said, a smile on his lips.

With his arms still around her, Persephone led Hades toward the dock. They had a ferry to catch.

Goodnight, Madison

SHE CALLS OUT FROM THE DARK WOODS, ASPENS BONE-WHITE against her frilly pink dress. Ice green river surges against Colorado's thick, cobalt darkness. Distant crunch of brush, like the snapping of bones, echoes along a path snaking toward the river bank. Toward the Animas—River of Lost Souls.

Toward Madison—my baby girl. "I'm here, Daddy! I'm here!"

It's always the same dream and I won't let it go. Not until I find her.

Her face shifts in the darkness, big, soulful blue eyes turning emerald green. Wind-blown strawberry blonde curls shifting into long, white-blonde ponytails. She clutches a silver chain, crystal heart dangling. The necklace I gave her.

Wear my heart against yours and I'll always protect you, I told her. She drops it into the river.

I failed. I failed her!

"He'll take more, Daddy," Madison says, green eyes bright with fear.

The dream shifts as Madison appears in the front yard, ponytails bouncing, shiny pink ribbons trailing like streamers. She twirls around in her frilly pink dress and white canvas sneakers, untied laces dragging the grass.

Eight feet from the front door.

Footsteps pound in my ears. The sound moving toward Madison.

I throw open the front door and the world shifts to wilderness. To the river winding past Durango. River banks and trails I knew so well.

Madi laughs, twirling in her pink dress as a dark figure lurches toward her.

My legs are lead, pumping hard, feet pounding the trail, tree line dark and dense. I can't. Get to her. In time.

"Run, Madi!" I shout. "RUN!"

Soupy, thick air tangles around me. I can't move. Can't run! She's only eight feet away from me. I lunge for her. Feel her warm hands against mine.

A shadowy figure grabs her from behind. Her soft little fingers slide like silk through my hands. I can't hold on!

Her shrieks echo against the river's churn as I stare at my empty hands. "Save us, Daddy," she whispers in my ear.

Madison, no! I wake up screaming. Again.

<hr>

Bleary-eyed after three hours of sleep, I stepped into the kitchen, dressed for work after a quick shower. Shaving could wait. It was still dark when I turned on the coffee maker. It rasped and sputtered, warm coffee scent comforting as the first trickle of coffee filled the pot.

I glanced at the kitchen table, the silhouette of my wife, Jess, sharp against the drawn curtains, startling me. We'd slept apart since Madi was taken. Five days, fifteen hours, and—I glanced at the time on the microwave—twenty-two minutes ago.

Right from my front lawn with an entire neighborhood watching. With cars driving past. Jess was eight feet away, inside for two minutes to grab the ringing phone. And me, her police officer dad asleep on the other side of the window.

Two minutes. Two fucking minutes to lose the best thing in my life, the light in my eyes. My bright-faced, innocent little seven-year-old, one front tooth missing, her whole life ahead of her.

Snatched right out of the yard.

After all the crying and praying and blaming, our eight years of marriage was little comfort right now. We'd been such a great team when Madi was born. Jess on inputs. Me on outputs and 3 a.m. feedings. We'd taken our turns walking the floor with Madison for hours when she was sick. Sharing the pain and the load as she grew. We'd been good then. But grief had a way of turning everything to shit. Of pushing two people away into their own little silos of hell.

I filled my mug with strong black coffee and took a bitter sip. It burned my tongue. Jumpstarting my burnt-out brain.

I'd promised to kick the soccer ball with Madi that day—after a quick power nap, I promised.

I winced, biting back the bum in my dry eyes. It was the first promise to her I'd ever broken.

Coffee mug in hand, I walked over to Jess. She stared past the curtains, eyes red and swollen, tears streaking her face. Bottle of vodka set next to the teddy bear mug (that Madi made for her at school) cradled in her hands. I leaned down and kissed her, sweet stink of alcohol on her breath. Her mug didn't have coffee in it. Just vodka.

She didn't move. Didn't glance at me. Was she blaming me or herself today for Madi's disappearance? It changed with the hour.

Either way, it was a blanket of silence between us. Growing thicker and heavier with every day Madi was gone.

"Be home late," I said with a hoarse rasp.

Jess nodded, tears threading down her face. Her lips trembled as she nodded toward me and pressed the coffee mug to her lips.

I rubbed her shoulder, feeling that bond between us slipping. Slipping away from me, from us. I felt numb, empty. Just couldn't squeeze another drop of compassion out of the tube for her or anyone today. I was broken. Without Madison, was there still an *us*?

I opened the front door and stepped outside toward my green pickup truck. I slid inside, started up the engine, and closed the door.

Screeching metal pierced the quiet, a garage door ratcheting open. Chains rattled, metal rasping. I winced, covering my ears until it was quiet again. My neighbor, Hal Masters. Had five kids, flipped cars he bought at auction. Repaired them in his driveway. Had old transmissions, engines, and tires stacked beside the garage. Madi played with two of his kids who always smelled like burnt oil and gasoline. Guy loved to talk. Cornered me at the mailbox some nights, hating on cops who had it in for his boys, crazy liberals, his ex-wife, and the government. Guy still didn't know I was a cop.

Wish he'd fix that goddamn garage door.

His burnt-orange Dodge Caravan with one white quarter panel lurched out of the garage and stopped. Horn honked, van idling as four dark-haired kids filed out the front door and climbed inside. The garage door screeched shut, like the gates of hell grinding closed, and the van backed into the street and drove off.

Loud rumble to my right drew my attention. God, my neighbors were noisy!

Jack Marten, my fifty-something neighbor, pulled into his driveway in a rusty silver Ford Econoline van. Hadn't washed the dirt and mud from it in the three years he'd lived next door. Nice enough guy. Quiet except when his grandkids visited. We only spoke on trash days. About the weather. His stroke. Cost of trash pickup. Shoveling snow. His twentysomething daughter.

I stared at the soccer ball greying in my dull winter lawn, right where Madi left it that afternoon, underneath my bedroom window, and swallowed the knot in my throat.

My cell phone rang.

"Landry," I barked, pressing the phone against my shoulder as I clicked my seatbelt in place. "Sam! Turn on your radio!" My partner, Declan Webber, his excited voice burning through

me. He lived one street over in this sprawling neighborhood of cracker box houses teeming with little kids and working parents.

"Why?"

"A 920F just came over the radio, buddy! Ambulance en route to Mercy."

My heart rose into my throat. Found child! I bit back the moisture stinging my eyes, whisper of hope in my ears as I gripped the steering wheel.

"Is it a girl, Dec?" I asked, afraid to hope. I couldn't wait for a drive to the hospital. I had to know. Now.

"Yes. I contacted Dispatch to be sure," said Dec. "En route to Mercy. Meet ya there."

"On my way."

I threw my phone into the passenger seat and slammed the stick into reverse, tearing down the driveway. I shifted the old truck's gears, clutch creaking and barreled down the highway heading southeast from Durango.

Toward Mercy Regional.

Dec met me at the elevator. Tall and lanky, with greying brown hair and sharp features, Dec patted my shoulder when I stepped out onto the restricted floor. We walked down the pearly white hall in silence, my heart pounding into my throat as we drew closer to the room at the end. Fluorescent lights scalded the crisp white walls and pooled on the tiles as we reached three officers outside the room. Their dark blue uniforms were bright against the intense overhead light.

Was it Madi? I couldn't think straight.

My hands shook, my mouth desert dry. The air smelled like warm citrus. I shoved my hands into the pockets of my black jacket, khakis swishing, yellow necktie too tight as I held up my badge to the officers.

"Sorry, Landry," said the officer in front of the room, "area's restricted." "Just a glance," I said, insistent. "Please."

"Look," said the stocky, dark-haired sergeant, "I know your kid's missing, Landry, but we've got dozens of missing kids everywhere. You know we gotta follow procedure. So, please—step back and let us do our job."

Rubbing my hand over my face, I stepped back, fighting the frustration, the anxiety churning.

Dec was at my shoulder, squeezing, supportive, protecting. Dec. We'd been through a lot together. Stakeouts, car chases, all-night report filing—each other's weddings. I'd been there when his twelve-year-old son's appendix burst. When his wife, Stacey died of cancer. When he'd made detective. And remarried.

I turned away, not looking him in the eye, staring at my feet instead.

With hands on my hips, I moved back from the door, trying my damned best to hold it all back, hold it all inside.

"Landry," said the sergeant, his voice quiet.

I turned around. The sergeant grabbed my arm and pulled me between the other two officers.

With his left arm, he gripped the door handle, pushing it wide open.

"I hope you understand I can't let you inside. We have to follow procedures."

There, in the bed, draped in blankets and tubes lay a little girl—seven or eight. Strawberry blonde curls tangled around her tanned, freckled face.

My heart broke into a million pieces and I swallowed my rage, forcing it down, burying it. It wasn't Madi.

"Thanks, Sergeant," I said, voice broken as I patted his shoulder, hands in my pockets.

I couldn't look him in the eye. Tears clouded my vision as I ran down the long, white hallway, Dec shouting my name.

<hr>

An hour later, I showed up at the precinct, Dec at his desk. He jumped up when I walked into the small office we shared.

"Sam, I'm really sorry," he said, his voice shaking. "Shouldn't have followed my gut. You okay?"

I started to tell him I was anything but okay, but his cell phone lit up, the wife's ringtone crackling through the room.

"Dammit, Camille," Dec snarled. "I don't have time for this right now."

Grumbling, he slid his phone out of his pocket, silencing the insistent ringtone, and returned to his desk. "Camille, I told you, I can't talk right now."

I hung my jacket by the door and sat down at my desk, logged into the computer, and opened my mail. Clicking through the network shares, I opened a folder with all my case files and reports. I searched for every report of missing area children in the past two weeks, looking for anything that might bring my daughter home.

"Wait, whoa—slow down, honey," Dec replied, his voice getting louder in the small blue office. "Camille, slower...whattaya mean come home now?" A long pause, Dec shook his head, ear glued to his cell phone, pale blue eyes wide. "I can't understand what you're saying. Wait, what? Gone? What do ya mean gone?"

The color fled from Dec's face, fear rising in his eyes. "Camille! Where's Ava?"

My stomach dropped into my feet. No, it couldn't be. His daughter, Ava. She was a year older than Madi. Rode the same bus as Madi to school every day. Where she should be right now.

Search data rolled across my monitor, displaying every disappearance in the Durango area.

Seven-year-old Kaitlyn Brooks' disappearance caught my eye, daughter of the Prosecuting Attorney, Trevor Brooks. No wonder his office hadn't responded to my emails. She'd disappeared seven days ago.

Two days before Madi.

Face ghost-white, Dec set down his cell phone, grabbing the desk phone in his fist, fingers flying across the buttons.

"Dispatch. Code 920C. Amber Alert initiated. Send hot response to Elkhorn Estates..."

I got to my feet, rushing over to his desk, but the lime green envelope in my inbox distracted me.

It looked suspicious. No return address. Detective Landry written in thick, black capital letters. Shaky script that slanted left.

Grabbing blue latex gloves from the box on my desk, I slid them on and opened the strange envelope. A single piece of lime green paper inside. More shaky writing.

Because of you, I buried my son. Soon, you'll know how that feels, Detective. All of you will.

Very soon. Time's running out. 24 hours 'til it's time to say goodnight, Madison.

For a moment, I couldn't breathe.

My brain swirled with eight years of cases and collars and testimonies. I could think of several people who wanted me dead. But killing a kid? That took a special kind of degenerate.

I turned toward Dec, letter in my gloved hand, and that's when I saw it. A chill blew across my heart.

A lime green envelope stuck out of Dec's inbox.

———

THE CRIME SCENE INVESTIGATION AT DEC'S HOUSE WAS A HORRIBLE *DÉJÀ VU*. One street behind me. Same Durango neighborhood. Same cracker box house. Cream, burgundy trim. Every inch of house, front yard, back yard, bus stop one house down was examined. Every bit of evidence scoured, tagged, bagged, and chain of custody logged. Neighborhood canvas. FBI. County. State. Mountain of paperwork. All the same motions all over again. With the same result.

No leads. And the clock was ticking down.

———

BACK IN THE PRECINCT, DEC AND I TRIED TO BE DILIGENT, thorough investigators, but with the stakes so, so personal it was impossible. We weren't officially working the case, but we were on it just the same. And wouldn't stop until our daughters came home.

Around 6 p.m., Trevor Brooks, La Plata County Prosecuting Attorney, walked into our office and shut the door.

He looked sick, exhausted, eyes filled with pain as he sat down in front of my desk. "Sam, Dec," he said, voice slow, tired.

Trevor had prosecuted a lot of cases in the county, including the eight years of cases Dec and I brought forward. There was talk of him running for Colorado's governor in a few years. But not everyone liked the tough prosecutor's style. The same person that wanted Dec and I both to suffer.

He took something out of his black suit pocket and laid it on my desk. I jumped up, Dec beside me.

"I saw the letters you received in evidence," said Trevor, pointing at the plastic bag containing a lime green envelope and single page note. "Thought you should see this one, too."

Same words. Same handwriting. Kaitlyn's name misspelled. "The 920F this morning," I said. "Your daughter?"

Trevor nodded. "Kaitie's stable, but hasn't woken up yet. Plenty of evidence pulled though. Mud from her clothes, cottonwood leaves, pine needles, dirt under her nails—in her hair. Wish she could tell us something." His voice broke and he paused a moment. "This note ties our three daughters' cases together. We've got every able body examining soil and plant samples, court case records, police reports—everything."

"What we need is the connection between us," I said. "What ties the three of us together?" I'd already been through my entire case file, searching for clues, connections—miracles.

Time was running out.

I had to find Madi before this monster's deadline. I had to. "Where'd they find Kaitie?" I asked.

Dec was a million miles away, trying to listen, trying to search.

"Cyclists found her unconscious, covered in dirt off 250. Near Baker's Bridge."

My brain raced. County Road 250 tangled like a shoelace across the many bends and turns of the Animas River. She'd claimed many a lost soul. *Had she claimed two more? Think, Landry, think!* So many trails and hills. Climbers and kayak rentals. Rafting the rapids. So much terrain—too much to cover.

I thought back to the scenes from the nightmare. Winding river. Aspens, white firs—spruce. River banks tangled with hawthorn and raspberry bushes. It wasn't a picnic area, not touristy or well-traveled. It felt wild and isolated.

Was Madi somehow showing me the way?

I paced the small room, arms crossed. "Trevor, I've been through all the cases connecting us, but nothing stands out."

"To us. One of these cases turned someone into a vengeful monster. We've got to find it, but it'll take time." He glanced at the letter on my desk. "Time we haven't got."

"Dec? Anyone come to mind? Someone who'd do something like this?"

Dec leaned forward in his chair, fear burning in his eyes. "Lots of DUIs, minor drug busts, B and Es, assaults. A few hit and runs, handful of murders, some armed robberies and aggravated assaults. Nothing stands out."

This was personal. Whoever did this didn't care about consequences. "This is someone who lost a child," I said.

Trevor glanced at Dec and then me. "Why do you say that?"

It was some of the worst pain I'd ever felt and I could see it in someone's eyes without even looking now. In that brief note, I'd felt it in the words, in the planning of this crime. Someone wanted us to feel the loss like they had.

"It's there, in the notes," I said.

"So, a case we're all connected to that resulted in someone losing a child?" Dec said in a shaky voice.

I nodded. "Gotta keep looking."

Trevor moved toward the door. "The FBI lab's identifying the manufacturer of that green paper and where it's sold in the area. My office is reviewing cases from the last decade. Back to my all-nighter." He opened the door. "Don't lose hope. If Kaitie wakes up tonight, I'll contact you."

"Trevor, you said something about cottonwood leaves," I said. He nodded. "They found some in her hair."

There were a couple types of cottonwoods that only grew near streams and rivers. I remember my grandpa pointing out old growth trees on fishing trips along the Animas. Cottonwoods, said they only grew in wetlands. Was called narrow-something.

"Find out what kind of cottonwood, would you?" Trevor frowned. "Why?"

"Because there's a couple types that only grow on riverbanks," I replied. "On it," Trevor said and left the office.

Maybe finding Kaitie was our first lucky break?

<hr>

For hours, I ran through all our collars, looking at every report and every conviction. Lists of names, stacks of manila folders. But I kept going back to one case that stuck with me.

Bertram. John David Bertram. Nineteen years old. Misdemeanor drug possession (before legalization) for cannabis. Third offense. Was one of my first drug busts. An early collar with Dec—before I made detective. I remembered that kid, a little on the small side. Harmless, a little lost. Drifted around Durango and the county, busking for money along the highways. Until the drunk and disorderly call that night.

Bonfire party out of control. Underage drinking.

Turned into a huge brawl. Lots of arrests that night, John Bertram among them. Kid went to jail for a year, three thousand in fines. At every court appearance, I remembered the quiet, shadowy presence of his old man in the back of the courtroom, first one out the door when court adjourned.

I looked up the kid in the inmates' database. My fingers went cold as I read his status: deceased. I opened the attached prison report. About the riot. My stomach dropped. Kid got shivved—two weeks before his release date. Bled out before they got him to Mercy.

Damn. I pushed back from the desk, rubbing my face. Kid was just nineteen. Had his whole life ahead of him.

Moving back to the computer, I searched for a death certificate, who claimed the body. Sally Bertram, mother. Jack Marten, father.

Stunned, I stared at the screen, rage mixing with grief. Jack Marten was my next-door neighbor.

With search warrant in hand, Dec and I went silent response to the neighborhood. The sun had already set, twilight settling against the houses as we rolled up at Marten's place, stopping behind his silver van.

Backup unit was already en route as I pounded Marten's front door, badge out, Glock 22 drawn. Dec went around the house to the back door.

"Detective Sam Landry, Durango Police Department. I have a

signed search warrant to search the property, including all vehicles. Open the door, Mr. Marten. Now."

Windows were dark, not a sound from inside the little yellow house.

I reached down and turned the doorknob. It clicked, door creaking open.

Again, I identified myself and the warrant I held, but not even a whisper echoed through the dark, silent house.

I stepped inside, sliding out a flashlight. I panned it through the dark house, Glock in hand. The air smelled like burnt oil.

Flashing my light around the dark kitchen showed flecks of ash all over the floor, scattered across the top of the gas stove. Papers lay on the kitchen counter. I flashed my light on them, my breath catching.

A map of the Animas River between Durango and Silverton, its center burned away. On the edge, something written in shaky black letters.

Detectives Landry and Webber:

My son, John, died because of you. Now, your children will die because of you. I've burned the only map. You won't find them in time.

Burn in hell, both of you.

"Dec!" I shouted, running for the front door. My phone rang as I stepped outside. Trevor.

"Landry, what'd you find out, Trevor?" I asked as Dec raced around the house toward me. "You were right, Sam," said Trevor. "The leaves came from a Narrowleaf Cottonwood."

The river in my dreams. It was the best damned lead I had right now.

CHASING THE FLIMSIEST LEAD I'D EVER FOLLOWED, I convinced Dec to follow me north, out to Bakers Bridge. Madi and Ava only had twenty-four hours. I hoped the twenty-minute drive wasn't wasting time we didn't have.

The search of Marten's van turned up nothing but mud and a shovel. Garage was empty except for one motorcycle helmet and a nail on the wall. Investigators were still scouring the house for evidence. An APB was out for Jack Marten, apprehend on sight.

With thermal imaging cameras and flashlights, Dec and I trekked along the Animas River's trail system north of Durango and Hermosa. Where they found Kaitlyn Brooks.

It was dark, thermals showing elk foraging and some raccoons and fox squirrels as Dec fanned out toward the tree line.

I moved along a path beside the river bank. Near fragrant firs and pines. Twigs snapped in the distance. Where Dec had gone.

The ground was soft and muddy, moon on the horizon, washing everything in eerie silvery purple light, temperatures dropping. Tangles of hawthorns and raspberry vines lined the path ahead.

Save me, Daddy, the voice whispered in my ear.

My breath quickened, legs heavy. I moved closer to the tangled vines along the trail.

Ahead, Ponderosa pines and white firs cast thick shadows across the gnarled stand of raspberry vines. That burgeoned with berries in August. A place only locals knew. Ringed by aspen and river birch leaves swayed, their bleach-white trunks protruding from the ground like bones.

Something rustled.

I turned.

A fox trotted across the path, disappearing into a thicket. I turned back toward the path.

The shovel struck me in face, knocking me to the ground. Flashlight fell out of my hand.

Everything shifted.

Eyes watered. World darkened. I felt for my Glock. Gone!

A dark figure moved toward the raspberry thicket, shovel in hand. A place only locals knew.

A place we wouldn't be found until the spring thaw.

On hands and knees, I dragged myself into the brush, fumbling for my phone. Dammit! No signal.

I struggled to my feet and whistled a shrill note. *C'mon, Dec!*

Boots thumped toward me.

I slid to my belly. And froze.

An unknown voice mumbled, searching, batting at the thick foliage. I held my breath. Until the sound moved past the brush.

At a distance, I followed the lean shadow as it lumbered beneath the moonlight toward a ring of trees. And several more, huge raspberry bushes.

Soon, a shovel thunked against soil, sifting it onto grass. I crept closer. Each step measured.

With every hiss of soil hitting grass, I slipped closer until the clearing came into view. I held back a tree limb, a cottonwood, I realized from the wisps of muddy cotton among the fallen leaves.

I peered into the clearing ringed with raspberry bushes and trees. Into a hole.

Six feet deep, a large wooden box inside. My heart slammed into my rib cage. Big enough for at least two children. Every hiss of shovel and whisper of soil covered the wooden box.

Burying it.

I pressed my soul up past my ribs, right beside my heart, ready to offer it in exchange for this monster's life. If I opened that box and didn't find Madi and Ava breathing, I'd end this bastard with my bare hands.

Spongy damp leaves absorbed my footsteps.

Thunk and snick of the shovel hollow, steady as the distance between me and the dark figure closed. Ten feet.

Seven feet.

Somewhere behind me, a shrill whistle arced through the treetops. Answering me. I grinned.

Dec. Headed this way.

With silent steps, I edged forward. Closer.

That's when I realized—the shoveling had stopped.

The figure—a man—was beside me now. Flashlight's bright beam blinding me.

Something slammed into my right leg. I fell backward through the brush and onto the river bank.

That wasn't a flashlight.

Horrible pain throbbed through my body. Bastard shot me with my own gun.

"Should have stayed down, son," said Jack Marten, standing over me now, ashen greyish brown hair flat against his face, grey stubble becoming a beard.

I stared up the barrel of my own Glock as it trained on my face. "This makes no sense, Jack," I said in a quiet voice.

"Of course, it does," Jack snapped, glaring at me. "John needed help, not a prison sentence. Because of you and your partner—and that filthy prosecutor—John died in there! He wasn't even twenty yet! Had his whole life ahead of him until you and Detective Webber stole it all from him!"

Smiling, Jack smashed the barrel of my G22 against my throat. "And now, Landry, it's time to say goodnight to Madison."

"You bastard!" I snarled. "Where's my daughter? Where's Ava?"

Jack grinned, crooked yellowed teeth turning dark against his pale, thin lips. "When the prosecutor's daughter escaped, I had to move things up a bit." Jack's finger moved toward the Glock's trigger. "They're safe together in a nice wooden box. That I need to finish burying. Don't know how you found us, but I can't have you rescuing them and ruining everything, Landry."

Gunshot rang out. I gasped, grabbing my chest, but it wasn't my Glock. Jack Marten dropped to the ground.

Dec stood behind him, his Glock drawn.

I struggled to stand as Dec shouldered his pistol.

"Over here," I said, voice raspy as I crawled back through the brush, toward the partially covered box.

Dec was behind me now, crawling through the brush behind me. "They're in here," I said. "Help me dig them out."

With the shovel, hands, sticks—whatever dug the fastest through the dirt—Dec and I uncovered the wooden box. I wedged the shovel's edge underneath the box boards, prying one after the other up while Dec ripped them off the frame.

I launched myself toward the dark box, peeling away a brown fleece blanket. Beneath it, my beautiful little girl rubbed her bright green eyes and lifted her head up from the little girl curled beside her.

"Daddy?" she said, reaching out for me.

Tears ran down my face, my breath catching in my throat, as I lifted Madison out of that dark hole, still dressed in her pink faerie dress, and into my arms.

"Ava? Answer me! Please!" Dec called, stepping down into the box.

"Poppy!" she cried, tears streaking her face as she sat up, jeans and a green sweatshirt covered in dirt. Sparkly purple headband tangled in her hair. "Poppy, help me!"

Dec sat in the dirt, holding Ava in his arms and cried.

Madi wrapped her arms around my neck, holding me tighter than she'd ever hugged me before. Her crystal heart necklace, caked with dirt, hung around her neck.

"Daddy, I kept your heart close," she whispered. "To show you where I was. So you'd save me."

Something kept Madi and me connected. Somehow. The necklace? I didn't care as long as Madison was safe.

"I love you so much it hurts, Madi," I said, pressing my face against hers, my voice breaking. "I love you more," she said with a giggle.

For the first time in days, I'd again have the privilege of putting my beautiful daughter to bed. Only with her in my arms would I ever again say, goodnight, Madison.

Visage

SCULPTOR BENEDICT CAMMISH WAS ALONE IN THE STUDIO the night young Lord Sherrington's muse drowned in the Thames. Never had he been so captivated by another human being's suffering than he had with the curly-haired aristocrat grieving over the body of his dead mistress.

Soot mixed with cinder-smoke and London's pervasive rain, the September night air gritty as Benedict emerged from the catacomb of narrow, grimy streets surrounding the Royal Exchange (rebuilt after the Great Fire in 1666). Shouts and wailing hung above the ubiquitous stench of wet horses, dung, and death, drawing him across the cobbled street that ran along the docks in a never-ending thrum of clacking hooves and rattling carriages.

People drowned every day in the Thames, but those involving nobles were happy little accidents witnessed outside London's usual patent playhouses. Unexpected entertainment for its lowest denizens. But only mad King George decreed what was legitimate art in the Commonwealth these days. Everything else was unlicensed and illegitimate.

Benedict held a crisp white handkerchief daubed with linseed oil to his nose as he stepped over horse dung and raw sewage that ran in the nearby gutters and made his way toward the pier. He gagged at the stench from the churchyard poor's holes that clung to every- thing, like the clouds of acrid coal-smoke obscured the starry night sky and waxing moon.

Constables laid a delicate, auburn-haired woman on the musty, weathered dock like a porcelain doll in a window display. Even in death, she looked angelic with a serene smile as if she was in repose, awaiting her wings.

Beneath the bright, clear lamplight, her brocaded, powder-blue gown pooled like a smear of Cheshire summer sky. It sparkled with celestial light, as if her soul had gathered up all the stars and dimmed the gibbous moon. Preparing to take flight.

Young Lord Sherrington threw himself across her lifeless body, weeping. His desperate, hoarse keening pierced London's din.

And fascinated Benedict.

"That's the Duke of Bolton's son," said someone in the crowd.

"An' his left-handed wife," a gruff, deep voice added.

Laughter rippled through the crowd.

The Duke of Bolton was once a popular poet in and around London and young Alastair Sherrington, third of four sons, was a talented poet in his own right. Royalty and commoners alike feasted on his tender love sonnets, his popularity already eclipsing his father's entire body of work. Or was it because the attractive young lord was a work of art that rivaled Michelangelo's David?

And according to his sonnets, the drowned woman was Lord Alastair's reason for living. Benedict hungered to experience such depth of emotion—even the pain of its loss— but passion had long abandoned him. Years of mentoring and ritualistic artistic development through London's patronage system had torn it away in tiny bits and crumbs until the vermin carried off the entire loaf. Leaving him an empty and numb sculptor with the world-renowned Visages Studio. Relegated to carving busts and statues for self-centered aristocrats and narcissistic patrons, he had little time for his own work. Nevertheless, these commissions allowed him to live comfortably in London's West End and work at the Royal Exchange.

At the cost of his art—and his soul.

Until Joseph Wright's amazing new painting shook Benedict from his stupor. The Corinthian Maid portrayed a young woman capturing the silhouette of her sleeping lover before he goes off to war. It was the final image of her lover, one that must sustain her for the rest of her days.

The painting changed Benedict forever. He longed to capture it in marble, but he lacked the passion to free it.

Like most artists, the world had never seen his true talent. The system passed over most artists, chewing them up and discarding them to make room for the season's chosen artist. Those artists spent the remainder of their careers carving bland, uninteresting-and sometimes, utterly homely-faces into the undeserving permanence of stone. Faces that looked as bored with their wealth and power as Benedict was with his station. Empty, vacuous faces that had no right to be remembered.

Now, he resorted to any means to gain meaningful commissions, including banal trickeries, bribery, and forays into the darkest arts. He'd just begun to realize that they had all intertwined to create something even baser than unoriginality and lies.

They created a monster. And it was a masterpiece.

Soaked and stinking of Thames sludge, Lord Sherrington clutched the woman's unresponsive body to his chest. Her smooth skin was bone-white beneath a layer of offal and grime, full lips blue, frozen green eyes empty-staring past him.

"Emilie, please!" Lord Sherrington lamented, shaking her, pumping her arms, and tilting her head back. "Open your eyes, Love! Emilie!"

His clubbed, wheaten hair slid free of its black ribbon and hung in dripping curls as he held her. His ruffled white shirt was stained brown and missing buttons, lace sleeves torn and dripping with soupy Thames muck. Her long, fiery-red tresses, tangled with garbage, were like embers in the lamplight, her brocades and silks stained with excrement and dirt. In death, she was still perfection, shining above London's filth and decay.

Beauty forever frozen.

Young Lord Sherrington wailed, begging her to return to him.

Something about this Adonis-like young man grieving over the woman's haunting vis- age moved Benedict to drape his waistcoat around the grieving young lord and comfort him with a supportive arm at his shoulders.

"Milord, there's nothing more you can do," Benedict said in a soft voice, half-sincere half-whisper. "She's gone."

"No! NO!" he shouted as a constable spread a linen sheet over the dead woman. "Emilie, no."

"Your lover?" Benedict asked.

Lord Sherrington nodded. "To never look upon her face again is a hell I cannot endure."

His voice broke, tears running down his face as he sagged in Benedict's grasp. He fished a gin flask from his vest pocket and handed it to the shivering young man. Lord Alastair pulled a long draught from the silver flask and handed it back.

Such perfection. The face of a poet—a sculptor's dream. Strong, fine-hewn chin, elegant cheekbones, gently curving aristocratic nose, full lips, and Wedgewood-blue eyes. Tall and lean body, a thick tangle of curly blond hair softening his boyish face. His beauty alone had probably won the dead woman's heart, before she even knew he came from money. But she probably fell in love with his gentle manner, kind heart, and deep emotions—rare qualities in London.

Even in his prime, Benedict had been at best ordinary-in countenance and aptitude—so he refused to create a self-portrait. Being ordinary was a worse sin than ugliness. It was but a single step from invisibility.

"Perhaps I can help?" Benedict offered.

The young man stared at him through long, teary lashes and swollen eyelids. "How? With every passing moment, her light fades. Are you a physician?"

"Forgive me, milord," he said with a deep bow, "I am Benedict Cammish, sculptor in residence with famed Visages Studio."

"A sculptor with Visages?" Lord Sherrington asked, looking confused. "The studio in the Royal Exchange?"

Benedict nodded.

"Court artists and sculptors to the Houses of York and Lancaster. Chosen portrait artists to the Tudors and Stuarts. Just last month, Master Elliot was commissioned to paint King George."

The young man stepped closer, eyes narrowing. "Is this just a cruel jest? How can you help my beloved Emilie?"

"There are ways," said Benedict in a quiet voice, watching the young man's blue eyes brighten, pupils widening as he took in every word. "For this public conversation," he continued, glancing around the growing crowd, "let us discuss capturing her beauty in wax, if you'll permit me. Or bronze, if you have the coin."

Lord Sherrington's lips parted. "A death mask?"

Benedict nodded. "Yes, some say a dark art, milord, but there are much darker arts in my repertoire, I assure you. Expensive but invaluable."

He let the words wash over the young lord, allowing them to settle into his heart and mind. It was always the first step.

"With every moment that passes," Benedict continued, stepping closer, "the spirit moves farther away. If the distance becomes too great, return is-impossible."

Lord Sherrington's mouth hung open and he just stared.

The initial interchange was always the most difficult. Benedict knew he had to conquer the young lord's indecision quickly or there would be no chance at a commission. Or any gain.

"I grieve for your loss, milord. If you have need of my services, you will find me at Visages in the Exchange. My condolences." He bowed, patting Lord Sherrington on the shoulder. "Don't wait too long-or she'll be gone forever."

Benedict turned toward the street as a carriage careened past, its heavy, metal wheels slinging sewage. He hung back until the road was clear.

"Wait!" the young lord cried, rushing toward him. He grabbed Benedict's shoulder, handing him his waistcoat. "Can you really do this?" he asked finally.

Benedict raised an eyebrow. "Do what, my lord?"

The young lord leaned forward, mouth against his ear. "Bring her back to me?"

He sighed. "I will try. It's all I can promise. The rite is expensive, though."

"How much?" the grieving young man asked.

"One hundred gold."

"I'll pay it," he said with a hiss. "Anything. Just—bring my Emilie back to me." Benedict hesitated a moment, then nodded. "Have her body brought to my studio at once. The longer we delay, the worse our chances."

The young lord nodded and paid a man for a cart. Then he pushed Emilie's body behind Benedict and into the noisy maze of narrow, poorly lit streets.

Benedict pressed a handkerchief over his nose as they stepped over rat carcasses and horse dung, avoiding puddles of sewage and run-off from the slaughterhouses that ran into open grates along the dirty streets. The young lord gagged several times, unused to London's filth. Benedict knew he lived far from these dangerous streets, sheltered in some sprawling country manor.

No, this privileged lad was so naive, so trusting. Such poor judgment to go off with someone he'd just met into London's dark, crime-infested maze of streets.

If he'd felt anything at all, Benedict might have felt sorry for this wide-eyed young lord, just discovering the baseness of the world around him, its cruel indifference and unending greed. He would soon learn the depths of its depravity.

At last, they crisscrossed the edge of the Royal Exchange's sprawling expanse and entered a dark, dank alley leading into the back of Visages Studio.

Didn't this hauntingly beautiful young lord wonder why they were entering a renowned studio like Visages through a dark alley?

His blind trust made Benedict's bones ache. But only a moment or two.

"This way," said Benedict, directing him through the open door and along a dark, musty brick corridor toward an oil lamp at the end.

Mold clung to mossy grey bricks, a black stain against the bright green, frilly moss as Benedict's boots skittered along the slick, muddy path into a large room.

"Here, m' lord," he said, pointing at a long table draped in linen.

"Please, call me Alastair," said the young man.

His arms shook under the weight of his muse as he lifted her from the cart and carried her into a windowless workroom at the back of the studio. Several wooden tables and stools crowded the cavernous, rectangular room with cool slate floors. Shelving covered all four walls. Bright ceramic paint pots filled one shelf, the others stacked with pumice stones, clear glass bottles of various stone powders, rolls of linen and muslin, and brushes of all widths and sizes.

Another shelf held iron chisels of all sizes, delicate wax- and plaster-carving tools, and hewing and scraping tools. The wooden handles were worn and smooth from decades of use. Benedict kept his expensive tools locked away.

Several slabs of pure white Italian marble (worth a small fortune) stood in the far corner, ropes anchoring them to wooden pallets. Across the room, a blacksmith's fire glowed in the dim lighting. Beside it was an anvil and a wooden rack of tools, the air smelling of heat and soot and sweat.

Benedict eased the young woman out of the exhausted young lord's arms and placed her onto the linen-draped table. Lord Alastair collapsed on a wooden stool and laid his head against Emilie's shoulder.

"She grows so cold," he said with a moan. "Her body is like winter."

"Then we must hurry," said Benedict, draping his waistcoat over a stool and rolling up his sleeves.

He unlocked a metal strongbox beneath the table and removed a bundle wrapped in soft, oiled leather. Hammers, chisels, and delicate wax-carving loops made from the finest British steel and collected over a lifetime. He spread them out beside Emilie's somber, angelic form and lit an oil lamp that hung above the table.

But his attention strayed to her flawless young lover and he wondered how it felt to inhabit such a perfect body. He ached to run his sculptor's hands across Alastair's lean body, tracing taut outlines of muscles across his torso and chest, following the gentle curve of his back to the supple muscles and sinews shaping his thighs.

Had Michelangelo felt David's form in his hands, aching for release?

Benedict was desperate to possess this young nobleman. To inhale his youth and passion. To immerse his soul in this well of beauty and perfection that had awakened an insatiable ache to create. He yearned to rediscover the fiery force deep within his soul that burned white-hot and propelled him to sculpt against all the reasons why he should just quit. Against all the reasons the world would never allow him to be an artist and capture them all in smooth white marble.

Benedict took shears and began cutting away the young woman's blue gown.

"Have some decency, man!" Alastair shouted, blocking Benedict's reach.

"Alastair," he snapped. "We must prepare her body for the ritual or there is no hope of bringing her back. It's the only way." He pulled the shears away. "I'll stop if you prefer."

He held back a smile, enjoyment settling warm against his chest at Alastair's intense emotions, and did his best to memorize how anguish and grief settled its suffocating veil across the young man's mouth.

Alastair's voice quivered and finally, he bowed his head in sweet defeat.

Benedict continued cutting away the gown from the young woman's chalk-white skin that was becoming more and more like marble as the moments fled. The heavy gown fell away, ivory undersilks clinging to the nymph-like curves of her supine body. Without the spark of life in her eyes and the gentle thump of a heartbeat to warm her skin, his actions felt clinical even for a sculptor. Regardless, he committed the details to memory.

"I'll need our agreed-upon sum before continuing, milord," said Benedict, stepping away from the table.

"Yes, of course." Alastair gasped and dug through all of his trouser pockets, turning them inside out. "I seem to be missing my coin purse!"

"Wretched pickpockets," Benedict muttered. "I regret sounding so mercenary, but I'll need that sum within the hour. Before she reaches the point of no return."

"Prepare her," Alastair snapped. "I'll return with it. You have my word."

Benedict fumbled with his tools until the studio's back door slammed shut.

With Alastair gone, he put on the black robes and opened his text on necromancy. He turned several crisp parchment pages to the marked passages on body preparation and set a metal wash tub beside the table.

The grieving young lord was in no condition to witness bloodletting his lover and the other brutal preparations to follow.

Benedict recited the necessary chants, using a bone wand he made during his first trial. His second trial had earned him these robes along with this text and its myriad spells. He knew the risks in this undertaking and he had no desire to be burned as a witch, so he kept these obvious steps hidden from the public—especially his studio colleagues. The body drained slowly, dark red blood trickling into the pan at an achingly slow pace as Benedict continued the ritual. He dipped the bone wand into Emilie's cooling blood as he recited the next incantation exactly as prescribed. Necromancy was as much an art as poetry or sculpture, something he learned with every passing day.

He smudged the vital fluid on Emilie's cold forehead and chin, her left and right cheeks, and both breasts. The room stank with congealing blood until he added fragrant peppermint oil to the oil lamp.

Benedict drew in a sharp breath and broke through her rib cage, cutting out her heart.

With a seamstress' precision, he sewed up her chest, all but a six-inch pocket, and covered her with a linen sheet. As her left wrist dripped dark blood into the metal tub, he oiled the landscape of her body with aromatic sage and rosemary oils. Long, slender legs, small tapering waist, and ample breasts. Graceful, elegant neck, delicate collarbone, and ripple of ribs flowing toward narrow hips.

He continued the necromancy spell, using mortar and pestle to reduce her once-beating heart to a paste mixed with gypsum and bone dust-and sage oil infused with rosemary and dark magic. He combined the paste with warm water and Emilie's blood, stirring the plaster until it was ready for casting.

Reciting another incantation, he dipped linen strips in the warm, dark plaster, wrapping Emilie's face first. He moved to her shoulders and chest, wrapping and chanting the spell as he covered her body in linen strips, at last, halting the rhythmic tick of blood against metal.

The linen would take another hour to dry and form the wax-casting mold.

Exhausted, he dropped into a wooden chair and leaned against the wall, waiting for Alastair to return. Benedict had already set the wax over the blacksmith's fire to melt. He'd reserved the remaining blood—and part of her heart—for the last step of the reanimation process. All he needed now was a spark to activate the magic. A sacrifice from the streets- at young Alastair's hand.

Benedict laid a hand against Emilie's stomach, stiff now with plaster and linen, feeling the first tremors of life. Her skin was warming beneath the plaster of death he had mixed. From her wax image, he would carve her visage in stone.

He delighted in this new approach to sculpting that had finally stirred the distant well of passion within him. His senses fluttered awake, casting ripples across the deepening darkness in his soul. He felt alive again, felt the long-buried sculptor inside him rise and claw his way out of the grave. Once completed, the studio would be the first to display his new work in all its glory. Recognizing him as an artist for the ages.

Like Michelangelo and Raphael, he would be remembered.

THREE HOURS LATER, ALASTAIR LIMPED INTO THE STUDIO, grey waistcoat torn and one sleeve bloody. A deep gash bled across a fresh white shirt, staining his grey breeches. He took two steps and collapsed.

Benedict rushed to him, pulling the young lord into his arms and carrying him over to one of the linen-draped tables. He slid a roll of linen underneath Alastair's head as the young lord gasped.

"What happened?"

"Cutthroats assailed me." Alastair groaned, his Wedgewood-blue eyes bright—as if the sun lit them from within.

His eyes turned glassy, welling with grief as Benedict tended his wounds. He spread a cool salve across the jagged gash. Alastair's fair skin was smooth and otherwise unblemished. He bandaged the wound with clean linen, memorizing the fluid contraction of muscles and smooth ripple of sinews.

"You're too kind, Mr. Cammish," said Alastair in a ragged voice, despair returning. "Call me Benedict," the sculptor whispered. "Do–

you have the coin then?"

Alastair nodded, reaching a hand into his breeches' pocket. He retrieved a leather pouch and extended it to Benedict.

"Thank you, milord," said Benedict, accepting the pouch. "Rest now while I prepare the mold."

"Mold?" said Alastair, frowning. He propped himself up on one elbow.

Benedict nodded and turned to Emilie. "A casting in wax." With careful movements, he freed the plaster mold from her body. "Tell me about your fair Emilie," he said, tapping the dried linen molding and lifting it from the table.

"We met at fourteen," said Alastair, "and my life was never the same. She was my breath and my soul.my first light upon waking. My last thought before dreaming." Tears threaded down his cheeks. "She filled me with such intensity and passion that I had to channel it somewhere or go mad, so I put quill to parchment. And Emilie became my muse in verse and rhyme." A hollow laugh rattled through his chest. "And in bed."

Benedict carried the molding toward the blacksmith fire.

"What of marriage?" he asked.

Alastair's eyes darkened, his face turning pale. "We fought tonight," he said with sigh. "Father arranged for me to marry a Scottish noble—and her substantial dowry." He laid a hand to his cheek, wincing. "Emilie slapped my face. She ran into the crowd and was–accosted. Then everyone was shouting and pointing at the river." His voice was tight, a sob breaking free. "In an instant, she was—just gone."

Benedict laid the molding on a large stone in the center of an iron cauldron and applied a final layer of plaster. The mold pulsed with indigo darkness when he finished and waited for it to dry. It would not take long with the dark magic active.

An hour later, Benedict checked the plaster before donning heavy leather gloves. He lifted an iron pot of roiling, honey-colored wax off the fire and poured it into the mold.

"Am I too late, Benedict?" Alastair asked.

"There's still a chance—if the spell works," he said. "We'll know soon enough."

The young lord fell silent, brooding as Benedict poured two more pots of melted wax into the mold, filling it. It would take an hour or two to harden. He returned his attention to the desperate young lord. So fair of face. Such a deep, resonating spirit. He sighed. Such a shame.

"There is one more thing. Dear Alastair." He ached to possess this young man, wanting to wear his young body over his aging, empty–ordinary–form.

Alastair's eyebrows quirked up, bow-shaped mouth pursing into a grimace.

"What else must I do?" he asked, exasperated, a deep weariness in his voice.

If Benedict had any compassion, he might have spared him one last trial, but it, too was empty.

"An act of violence, milord."

Alastair sat up, staring at his beloved beneath the linen sheet. At last, death whispered softly to him from the flicker of oil lamps, a hint of peppermint soothing the chill of night settling against his skin. The young lord began to shake, at last understanding the finality of his loss.

Benedict had seen this look many times over the years, had watched death's familiar second act up close from grand box seats and from a distance. But no matter where act three played, the drama always ended the same way-illegitimate or not.

Like the theatre—and all art—there was something elegant and graceful about the reciprocity of life and death. Something young Alastair was about to discover.

"I don't understand," Alastair said with a heavy sigh as he stood up.

"The magic works on reciprocity," said Benedict, turning away. "To infuse life, we must—take it from somewhere. A reciprocal death. The energy is the catalyst for reanimation. To call back her spirit. Do you understand?"

Alastair's face darkened, a shattered look in those Wedgewood-blue eyes that burned with indecision. And horror. "Are you asking me to commit murder?"

Benedict pulled back the sheet covering Emilie. Pasty white skin glowed in the lamp light, illuminating the jagged incision between her firm, round breasts and large, celadon-green eyes that were open and staring past this world.

She was a mold ready to fill, a wick ready to light.

"Like this murder, milord?" Benedict shouted. "Attacked and drowned before your very eyes! The man responsible escaping into London's filth!"

Alastair looked away, eyes misting. "What must I–do?" he asked finally.

"Bring me a beating heart."

Benedict watched the horror well anew in the young lord's eyes. Warring against the shreds of humanity Benedict had left him, already unraveling as Alastair's lips pressed into a thin, quivering line, the words settling into the sharp, heavy silence.

"Or one moment after its last beat," said Benedict. "Without it, the best I can offer is a death mask of your beloved Emilie, milord. Nothing more."

Turmoil warred across Alastair's face and clung to his limbs like a heavy, ill-fitting shroud. In his head, Benedict sketched the cursory lines and angles of Alastair's portrait, capturing every curve and depth of emotion haunting his face, hollowing his cheeks, and igniting his soft blue irises into blue flames.

"Perhaps you can find something worthy to trade for it in those filth-ridden streets?"

Alastair stared at his beloved, the ache of indecision shadowing his face as the last threads of morality dangled from his fingertips.

"It's all right, Lord Sherrington," he said. "I understand. We shall proceed with the mask instead then."

Benedict sighed and moved toward the wax-filled mold hardening beside the blacksmith's fire.

"Wait!" Something dark crouched in Alastair's voice, threads slipping free at last. "I'll get the heart."

The words came easily this time and Benedict made note of it, acceptance coloring the young man's movements with a dark fluidity and strange lightness of step that invariably followed as Alastair slid on his waist- coat and bled into the night in search of prey.

His first, Benedict knew.

The first anemic rays of light clawed at East End's cinder-smoked sky, the haze settling on jagged rows of spindly hovels wedged together with crumbling brick and brittle timber. Gritty air stank with coal dust, refuse, and unburied corpses in the churchyard. In the wake of another sickly dawn that moved the year another day closer to winter, jagged black shadows still wrapped the studio's narrow alley in quiet darkness as Lord Alastair Sherrington returned.

In his bloodied fist was a fresh human heart.

The absence of civility was total in the young noble's eyes, peeling back generations of domestication and grooming that made man king over the beasts of field and forest and gave him compassion for his fellow man—keeping him from becoming a monster.

Gone, like the extinguished sparks in his muse's dead eyes. In three acts, Benedict had returned this cultured young aristocrat to the wild. Reducing him to his most savage form.

Benedict smiled. For art.

He accepted the heart, noting the young man's torn sleeves and ripped waistcoat spattered with fresh, new blood. He approached Emilie, bone wand in hand as thin tendrils of first light streamed into the room through the shoddy roof as Benedict spoke the final incantation from the definitive treatise on reanimation.

Alastair hung at his left shoulder, feral gaze locked on Emilie's face.

The young lord didn't even flinch when Benedict wedged the freshly harvested heart into the pocket he'd sown into Emilie's chest. When the heart was in place, Benedict laid his hand over the incision and chanted a verse. The final verse.

In the new day's first pallid grey rays of sunlight, something returned to Emilie's eyes. Writhed behind them, dull sheen of death receding at last.

Joy danced across Alastair's face, the mask of despair lifting, a smile touching the corners of his mouth. Feral. Hungry at last.

"Emilie?" he cried, tears brimming in his tired, faded blue eyes.

She struggled to speak, but only a squeak came out, her lips moving.

Alastair flung himself against the young woman, sobbing and

muttering unintelligible words as the rise and fall of breath returned to her lungs. The flicker and glow of life lit her eyes like relighting a candle.

But the wick was always shorter and a little burnt, the light duller than before. Washed out.

"Thank you," Alastair cried, grabbing hold of Benedict's hands, shaking them. "Thank you!"

Benedict just nodded as Alastair gathered the young woman into his arms and draped her in linen. He escorted Lord Sherrington and his undead muse into the alley and an awaiting carriage. He covered his nose with a linseed-oil-daubed handkerchief and watched the carriage lurch across the cobblestones, heading out of London's filth. Toward his father's estate.

Poor Alastair had no idea Benedict pick-pocketed him earlier that evening.

He returned to the studio. His colleagues would arrive soon. He needed to finish the wax casting., his guide for her marble sculpture. And he needed to sketch intimate drawings of young Lord Sherrington, his muse. His David in marble. Both works would take time and bring him lots of coin.

After all, great art took time. It required great suffering. And suffering paid lots of coin.

Like fathers paying handsomely to drown muses in the Thames and force their sons into arranged marriages—and out of poetry.

Alastair was young. The Duke assured him the young lord would forget his mistress and his sweet little sonnets in Scotland. Keeping the Duke's poetry more popular—and his son's forgotten.

Benedict forgot to tell the Duke that he charged extra to reanimate muses, but creating monsters was a service he provided free of charge. Kept the violence behind estate doors where it belonged. Allowing heirs like young Alastair to suffer like a good little poet.

Nevertheless, Benedict was eager to read Alastair's next poetry book.

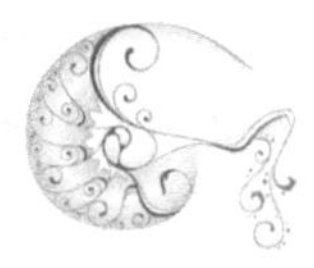

Speechless in Seattle

THUNDER RUMBLED THROUGH THE EVENING SKY AS STORM clouds rolled off Elliot Bay where Brant Trenerry stood in Kerry Park, staff raised, ready to change the world.

The air prickled with energy, alive with the swirling of ancient forces as he summoned the power of all the wizards who'd carried this staff before him. Already he smelled the acrid, almost electric tang of magic from the eye of the storm, a crisp, pungent odor that tingled his nose like cracked pepper.

He gripped the family staff tighter and whispered a spell he'd spent months crafting. It hissed from his lips, quickly joined by ancestral voices that echoed from the family grimoire he carried in the messenger bag underneath his cloak. He just needed to get the words right.

Brant was descended from House Trenerry, one of the five great houses of wizardry that had settled in Seattle's sleepy streets nearly two hundred years ago. They lived quietly alongside mundanes who couldn't see or hear the trappings of this magical world.

He'd spent his whole life studying magic, schooled in the Arts before preschool and throughout his time in public schools. He'd lettered in all three schools of magic and passed all of his MHAATs. A senior at Seattle's College for the Performance of Magical Arts, he had a

3.8 average in Calefaction magic and a 4.0 in both Camber and Compulsion minors.

After committing the important spells of House Trenerry's grimoires to memory, he scoured Seattle's streets for a familiar, like all wizards-to-be. Just last month, he'd enticed a winged, tortoiseshell cat named Zipestra into the role. She'd been following him since his twentieth birthday, but it took him nearly a year to convince her to accept him as her wizard. Originally, he'd nicknamed her pest for short, but the claw marks on his arm convinced him to choose Zip instead. *Cats.*

Now, on his twenty-first birthday, with his focus in place, he'd chosen a place of power to perform the spell. After the incantation, he'd inherit his house's power, becoming a full wizard in the eyes of the five great houses and Seattle's magical community.

If he completed the spell correctly.

All he had to do was say it.

He winced as he remembered his childhood struggle with stuttering. He'd grown out of it, but sometimes, when he was tired—or nervous— he stuttered.

Brant's staff glowed molten purple now, steaming in the mist-laden air, thrumming with pent-up forces ready for release. Carved out of myrtlewood on the steps of Glastonbury Abbey, honed with genera- tions of Trenerry blood, sweat, and incantations, this staff had weath- ered continents and centuries. An only child, he was the seventh generation to carry it—which worried his parents.

Lightning fractured the sky, casting a neon yellow flash against Kerry Park's tall, steel sculpture. *Changing Form*, by Doris Totten Chase, consisted of two boxes with spherical cutouts that framed the skyline like a portal. For Brant, it was the most powerful place in Seattle.

Touched by the Puget Sound, Kerry Park carried elemental powers of earth, wind, and water. It pulsed with the constant energies of thou- sands of people who walked these worn red bricks every day. The walk- ways writhed with the hopes and dreams of tourists snapping countless photographs through the sculpture's circle. Each time, the world changed; storing bits and pieces of its magic into moments scattered throughout the Internet, framed on walls, and printed in the media—

touching everything and everyone. It just needed a spark. An element of fire to focus all the power he was about to summon.

Thunder roiled around him as he chanted the spell louder. The wind rose, strafing his face with rain. He stumbled over a word, then carefully spoke it again. Brant's familiar fluttered around him, channeling his newfound energies into the staff, combining them into a single force. A task that familiars had performed for thousands of years.

The staff grew hot in his hand as lightning flashed overhead, crackling like pebbles against a tin roof. He shouted the spell's final line and slammed the end of the staff into the ground.

A massive fireball burst from the staff like a comet, shooting across the black, churning sky and exploding in a shower of sparks that rained down like fireworks. A jagged bolt of lightning tore across the horizon, thundering in a sharp, piercing clap.

Fire reigned from the clouds as a bright ring of flame rushed across the park, rolling over Seattle.

I'm free! It was Zip, his familiar's voice.

Brant turned, staring into the cat's deep copper eyes.

"Free?" he cried, shaking ashes out of his dark hair. "But...you're b-bound to me."

The winged cat rolled over in mid-air and stretched cream-speckled paws, arching her back as she clawed at the air.

Not anymore, Zip purred. *You spent so much time perfecting diction and crafting the spell, little wizard. You forgot about the words.*

"What are you talking about?" He glared at Zip as she licked her front paw. "I crafted my spell from the exact words in the Trenerry grimoire. And I didn't stutter!"

The pit of his stomach dropped into his feet. *What had he missed?*

Zip sighed. *That's the problem, little wizard. You forgot the first rule of magic: update all spells.*

He cringed, bristling at the smug, little furball. He wouldn't be lectured about magic by a flying cat.

A thousand years ago, each magical word was precise and had one meaning, Zip continued, rubbing against his elbow, her throaty purr soothing. *Today, those words have many meanings.*

He sighed and rubbed his forehead. "So what did I cast?"

You didn't call House Trenerry's magic into your staff, said Zip, *you set free every familiar in Seattle.*

Brant's eyes widened and he cursed under his breath. "I *what?* Oh, Gods, my father's gonna kill me! I've gotta fix this!"

He cast a Compulsion spell, transporting him to the one place that could help him, before anyone found out, The Seattle Library of the Hidden Arts.

WILLA ROSEWARREN PULLED HER LAVENDER CLOAK TIGHT, head down, auburn hair tucked behind her ears as she shuffled through the angry crowd of wizards gathered at the steps of The Seattle Library of the Hidden Arts. Thunder rumbled in the distance. She smiled, hoping the storm would clear out these protestors.

Luna, the white dove on her shoulder, cooed in soothing warbles. The familiar scrubbed the impurities from Willa's magic until her Calefaction burned a pure, white flame. The five houses had mastered all three schools of magic, but only House Rosewarren exclusively practiced Calefaction, the manipulation of heat and light. Their wizards were the best at it, too—not that Willa liked to brag.

Willa loved practicing magic, but she preferred managing the library's collections, assisting researchers, and gathering rare, magical artifacts for her Seattle patrons. As the newest librarian, two weeks today, she'd volunteered for the evening shift, hoping to learn about the evening crowd's needs. She'd expected it to be busy, but she never dreamed there'd be protests.

She glanced at the two stone griffins perched on either side of the winding granite staircase that curved toward the library's oak doors, but the glowing slashes of blue, green, and orange runes obscured her view.

She groaned. Wizard graffiti.

The air smelled like melted plastic as she read the symbols flashing in the evening air.

Tomes Belong in Libraries. Grimoires Shouldn't be Digitized! Barcodes are Bad Magic!

Willa sighed, brushing away the runes. They turned to dust and floated away. Wizards. She rolled her eyes. Perfecting the magical arts for thousands of years, yet show them a barcode and they start a witch-hunt. Five great houses competing against each other since the Bronze Age, but mention digitizing family grimoires and they all band together.

Lightning flickered to the west as she swerved past two wizards, a man with black hair and a sable-haired, dark-skinned woman. They wore the royal blue robes of House Negus as they burned runes into the air, chanting, "Barcodes ruin grimoires!" as Willa reached the staircase. One had a shaggy brown dog that panted and wagged its tail. The other had a red squirrel perched on her shoulder, happily shelling an acorn. Willa loved seeing all the familiars.

House Rosewarren built this white two-story, gothic revival in the 1850s. At times, the black mansard roof with its wrought-iron widow's walk looked forbidding, but the spandreled portico softened its harsh appearance. It sat in stark contrast to the modern curves of the Seattle Art Museum, just a few blocks from Elliot Bay. Mundanes couldn't see the building due to the extensive Camber magic that curved and refracted space around it.

A white-haired wizard dressed in a brown cloak and the yellow silk robes of House Kestell stepped in front of Willa. His familiar, a black stag, fidgeted beside him, rubbing its antlers against the granite stairs. The wizard smelled like stale smoke and decaying silk, his teeth clicking when he talked.

"This is an outrage!" he shouted. His features were sharp and hawk-like, small, dark eyes glaring. A goatee framed his angry pout as he shook a finger at her. "Just you wait until all the houses hear about what you've done here! It's desecration!"

A chestnut-haired sorceress wearing an orange pullover rushed out of the library, cupping blue orbs in each hand. "Have you seen my tiger?" she asked, looking upset, eyes glassy, a trail of blue sparkles trickling through her fingers and scattering down the steps.

Willa shook her head. "No, sorry."

She moved away from Willa. "Has anyone seen my white tiger, Freyja? Anyone? Please, my familiar's vanished! I can't focus spells without her!"

Distraught, she shuffled past Willa who tried to sidestep the angry

House Kestell wizard, but other protesters blocked her path, tossing fireballs at the stone griffins.

The griffins let out a screech, broke free of their magical tethers, and fluttered into the night, halting the protestors' shouts.

Willa gasped, nearly falling down the stairs. The Library familiars!

She grabbed the railing as Luna took flight, following the griffins.

The deathly quiet on the stairs forced her to turn around. Every familiar was gone.

"What's happened?" someone whispered. The wizards looked lost, staring at each other as the protest runes faded into puffs of smoke.

"Where's my dog?"

Storm clouds broke, rain pattering against the granite steps, washing away dust and smoke. Panicked, the wizards scattered.

Willa didn't know what happened to the familiars, but she'd start researching possible causes—and solutions. She pulled open the heavy oak door and collided with a man in a black cloak.

Everything turned dark when the young man's cloak tangled around her head and she fell. She struggled to free herself, but the marble floor was too slick and she couldn't get to her feet. She groaned in frustration as the man struggled up from the floor.

He pulled back the edge of his cloak. She stared up at him, studying his kind face, warm brown eyes, and wavy brown hair. He looked mesmerized, his eyes wide and unblinking. He was quite attractive, tall and slim, tousled hair just above the collar of his grey henley, and wide-set brown eyes like a distraught puppy. His cloak almost hid his faded jeans. She brushed a tangle of auburn locks away from her face and smiled, but he seemed almost frightened of her. His lips moved, but no words came out.

Instead, the young man signed a spell, copper flashes dancing across her body, lifting her from the floor. Sweat misted his face as he seemed to struggle to hold the spell until she was on her feet. She grinned. A wizard!

"Thank you," said Willa, struggling to catch her breath.

She straightened her cloak, smoothing the Juliet sleeves of her pale mint blouse. Her black pencil skirt was hiked up, so she straightened the seam. Her rain-damp face was flushed, cheeks burning as she did her best not to stare—or make him feel more uncomfortable. After all, as a wizard of House Rosewarren, it was her duty to uphold the house's reputation of producing helpful, compassionate wizards and good stewards of written magical knowledge.

At last, the young man returned her smile, looking calmer as he picked up his staff and bowed politely. But that distressed look returned to his face as he ducked into the east reading room.

Willa followed, hoping he needed help with his research.

"Can I help you find something?" she asked, hurrying down the long, narrow room, past wooden tables and brown leather couches. "I work here."

He turned away from a shelf of books against the far wall, smiling. "I...*thought* you were from House Rosewarren."

Bookshelves lined every wall, the room painted a pale aqua, and stood in neat rows of three between the tables and couches. The young wizard seemed fascinated by the rows of colorful books. Frosty white orbs floated across the ceilings in a slow, circular path, lighting the room with soft white light as he rushed from shelf to shelf, a look of desperation in his eyes.

Thick tomes and loosely bound manuscripts filled the shelves, some books glowing blue. Others had pictures that flashed along their spines, others adorned with shiny jewels and fiery runes. Leather, colored card stock, delicate silks, and vellums in frosty, crisp sheets.

He closed his eyes a moment, taking a deep breath, which seemed to calm him. Willa felt even more attracted to him now. He loved the smell of books. She was certain of it. When he opened his eyes, they had a dreamy quality, like someone who wanted to lose himself in every tome and text.

She breathed in the comforting scent of leather and old paper, knowing this man was someone she could have long conversations about magic and grimoires with over hot tea and scones. Someone who probably loved the rain and the ocean's nearness to the city. She desperately wanted to get to know him.

The wizard walked toward the large, glass summoning spheres in the corner that bobbed in the air at eye level. They were the size of large melons and had more facets than a diamond.

"What are you searching for?" Willa asked, startling him.

He reached toward the spheres and pictures danced across the clear glass. With a flick of his index finger, and a bit of Compulsion magic glowing lavender at his fingertips, he tried to use the spheres. He was probably new to the Library's new catalog system.

"Just say what you're looking for and the spheres will show you images from our collection."

"Familiars," he snapped.

Willa's eyes grew wide. No wonder he was distressed and struggling with his magic. He'd probably lost his familiar!

"Did you lose yours, too?" she asked.

The young man looked mortified now, his face pinching, mouth twisting into a grimace, eyes smashed closed.

Finally, he nodded and glanced at the shelves and the tomes, still looking for something. *Why didn't he just tell her what he needed? She couldn't help him if he wouldn't talk to her.*

"I lost my familiar, too, so I know how you feel," she said, touching his sleeve. He didn't pull away. "I'm here to help though. Just tell me what you're researching and I'll point you to the appropriate resources."

He stared at her in silence, a battle warring behind his eyes.

"I'm Willa," she said, extending her hand.

He pursed his lips. "Brant," he replied, his voice clipped. He smiled at her now. "You're from House Trenerry, aren't you?" she said as she approached the glass spheres. "I recognize the staff."

He nodded.

"There are volumes written on familiars, Brant," she said, returning his smile. "Our new online system should help narrow down our choices."

She chanted a Calefaction spell, a force that controlled heat and light, and focused it on the books.

Across the room, two massive tomes floated off the shelves, scattering dust and sparks as they moved toward her. They hung in the air to her right. One had glowing orange runes on the cover and the other had blurry images rushing across its face.

"Here are two volumes on the subject," she said. "They haven't been digitized yet." She smiled, pointing to three small runes that sparkled red on the spine. "But I've barcoded them so the new system can find and retrieve them."

"That's n-n-nice," said Brant. Embarrassment flushed his face and he turned away, gripping his staff.

"What's wrong, Brant?"

He pitched the staff at the leather couch. It bounced off and hung in the air for a moment. Then it clattered against the marble floor.

"It's m-my f-fault!" His face burned with shame. "The f-f-familiars." He squeezed his eyes closed, balling his hands into fists. "I—I bungled the spell. I would have...been a full-fledged House Trenerry wizard. But that w-won't happen n-now."

Willa winced at his comments, feeling terrible for him. Tonight was the poor man's birthday! All wizards received their full power on their twenty-first birthday, but something had gone wrong for him. She laid a hand against his arm.

"Tonight was your twenty-first birthday, wasn't it?" she asked. "You were summoning your power, weren't you?"

He nodded, gritting his teeth. "I didn't u-update the spell. My fault." He let out a frustrated growl.

"Is that what happened?" Willa asked, turning him around to face her. "You crafted your spell using the original House spell?"

He cringed, nodding again.

"Do you have your family's grimoire with you?" she asked. "The one containing both spells?" She needed to see the whole text, including the spell he'd crafted.

"Y-yes," he answered in a quiet voice as he lifted the heavy tome out of his satchel. The cover had a frosty sheen, inlaid with aquamarines and polished silver. It sparkled as he handed it to Willa who cradled the book in her arms.

She took his hand, flushing at the touch of his fingers against hers as she led him to the summoning spheres.

"I'll digitize the contents," said Willa. "Then we'll compare it to all known spells dealing with familiars."

She laid the book on a nearby table and summoned a crystal sphere. She pressed her fingers against its smooth surface, reciting a Calefaction spell that lit Brant's grimoire. The spell illuminated every page, every pen stroke, every indentation as the sphere shifted colors and hummed with energy. Words and symbols burned images into the air as they traveled out of the book and into the sphere, turning and spinning.

Heat from the symbols and the Calefaction spell warmed Brant's face. He looked panicked now, as if he were reliving their casting and Willa couldn't help but feel badly for him.

"Once we get the spells captured, I'll compare them to the familiars spell." She smiled at him. "Don't worry, Brant. We can fix this."

"Hope...you're right."

It took several long, painful minutes before the sphere finished and went dark. Only then did Willa approach it.

"Locate all spells dealing with familiars," she said to the sphere.

Images and symbols flashed over the sphere's misty surface, whispers hissing as the runic signs glowed in the air. Willa walked among them, studying the information. Brant joined her, his shoulder touching hers now. He smelled of spring rain and a clean, woodsy scent that clouded her brain for a moment as she leaned closer to him.

Willa pointed at a cluster of pulsating runes.

"Do you remember this part of your spell, Brant?" She smiled. "It's beautifully crafted. Such a nice balance of Camber and Compulsion that builds with power into the Calefaction summons at the end."

"Yes," he replied, his face flushed. "It was-was tough...to cr-cr-craft."

Willa lifted a grouping of blue runes from the sphere. They floated in the air to her left, four double-spaced lines. She recited another spell as she reached into the sphere, teasing out a group of gold symbols. Four rows of double-spaced, gold runes hung at her right shoulder. She glanced left to right, reading each symbol, comparing one against the other.

"There it is," she said in a quiet voice.

Brant moved toward the symbols, studying them in silence.

"The blue symbols are part of the original Trenerry spell you spoke tonight," she said and motioned to her right. "The gold symbols are the spell you crafted."

Brant reached out and gathered the gold symbols in his palm. He dragged them over to the blue symbols and dropped them on top.

Together, they compared the overlap of every symbol, the curve and brilliance of each one, blue against gold.

"Look for missteps," she said in a soft voice.

Brant nodded. "Right, anything that might have changed the spell's outcome or ruined the incantation somehow."

Brant's voice filled the room as Willa's spell called back the echo of his cast spell. The words floated through the world forever and she could call them back like a little capsule of time. She watched Brant wince at the sound of his own voice.

"My parents always w-worried about m-me," said Brant, bowing his head. "Guess they—they always knew I'd amount t-t-to n-nothing. That I'd n-n-never capture the energies of H-House Trenerry."

Willa's heart broke at his despair. She slid her arm around his shoulders. "Don't you talk like that, Brant! They believe in you and so do I. You *will* become a full wizard tonight. I just know it!"

At last, his face brightened. "Hope you're r-right, Willa." He paused a moment. "I s-stuttered as a kid, but now, only b-beautiful women make me s-s-stutter."

She couldn't hold back her grin as she watched him concentrate on the symbols again, studying the agreements in the magic. Looking for the green tint wherever the blue and gold symbols matched.

They stood in silence for a long time, studying the symbols, but finally, Brant cried out and pointed at three, tiny symbols that didn't match.

"Here—they are! Three symbols that broke the familiars' bonds," he said, pointing. "I used an old h-homonym from my grimoire." He sighed. "It strictly meant a wizard's talisman once."

Willa nodded. "Yes, you're right! That symbol's become slang for familiars. Any wizard might have used that symbol to mean staff, Brant."

"That damned cat's gonna gloat for weeks over my mistake."

Willa captured the three symbols, scattering the rest into a shower of sparks that dissolved in a puff of smoke.

"Show counter signs to this magical break," she said into the sphere. "Then show us the spell to re-forge our familiars' bonds."

"And focus only on the staff," Brant added.

Vivid purple letters appeared beside three gold symbols. Brant read through the line of purple symbols and then studied the three gold signs.

"That's the fix then," he said, his hands shaking. "I'll uh—recast with those symbols. But without my familiar, it won't work." He sighed in exasperation and kicked the leather couch.

Willa grabbed his arm as she turned toward the sphere. He didn't understand that he controlled the power he was summoning, not his familiar. Familiars were there for focus and tempering, nothing more.

She laid a crisp piece of blank parchment onto the table. With both hands, she lifted the symbols out of the air and pressed them against the parchment, a spell of Calefaction on her lips.

Her words were precise, the diction flawless as thin blades of fire carved Brant's eleven symbols into the parchment. She blew on the paper until it cooled and all the blackened edges had hardened. Then she rolled up the scroll and handed it to Brant. She loved the feel of his warm, strong fingers against her palm, wanting to entwine her fingers in his.

"There," she said. "You won't have to rely on memory."

With a loud thud, the library doors slammed open as dozens of wizards poured inside, demanding assistance. They brushed past Willa and Brant, making their way down the long hallway toward the library's main service desk. A big, round walnut desk stood in the center of the vaulted foyer. Four librarians cowered behind it as the herd descended on them.

A huge chandelier hung over the service desk, dripping with hundreds of multifaceted, teardrop crystals. Swirls of light danced across the cold marble floor as the growing crowd clacked across it, heaping themselves around the desk in tangles of three and four people deep. The roar of their voices echoed through the chamber. On either side of the round, ornate desk were two sets of wrought-iron staircases winding gracefully upstairs to special collections and more reading rooms. The two staircases met at the top in an elegant balcony overlooking the marble foyer. Brant eyed the balcony and Willa worried that he might jump from it.

"My familiar's just disappeared," someone shouted. "Now, I can't cast any spells! You've got to help me!"

"Please, my familiar's missing!" shouted another wizard. "I need that hawk to strengthen my Compulsion spells!"

Librarians huddled behind the desk, calling up tomes that flew off reading room shelves to the hands of Willa's colleagues who were desperate to help.

Brant tugged on her sleeve. "There's only one way to f-fix this. Will you. Help—me?"

Willa nodded. She was afraid he wouldn't ask. "Of course!"

Brant retrieved his staff and then folded her arm in his. He fought his way through the growing crowd of wizards, pulling her along until they reached Seattle's rain-swept streets.

———

BRANT SIGNED HIS WAY THROUGH A SERIES OF CAMBER spells that shifted and refracted space, allowing him to twist magical forces into a portal that brought them back to Kerry Park. He tugged her up the red brick stairs to the strange, steel geometric sculpture.

Through the steel's round cutouts, he gazed at Elliot Bay through a haze of blackness and rain-smeared city lights framing the Space Needle and Seattle's unforgettable skyline. The storm had passed to the east, clouds faded to wispy trails allowing stars to burn through the swath of midnight sky.

Brant lifted the staff toward the sky. He unfurled Willa's parchment that burned with the new incantation. Eleven symbols that would re-bond the familiars and make him Seattle's newest full wizard.

"Ready?" Willa called above the rush of wind.

She stood beside him, so encouraging, so inspiring. Maybe she'd see him as more than a stuttering fool?

Nodding, he gripped the parchment and the myrtlewood staff, staring at the fiery symbols. He whispered them, practicing each one.

Fear gripped him as he clenched the staff and cast the corrected spell. Only eleven symbols stood between him and his birthright. This time, he would get it right.

Brant cleared his throat and held the parchment out to Willa.

"Will you hold this while I cast?"

She nodded, taking the stiff parchment and holding it in front of him.

One last time, he ran through the spell in his head, pausing to insert the eleven corrected signs.

Then, concentrating on each symbol, Brant spoke the crafted spell with precision, working through each section with confidence. He felt the uneven flow of energy through him, untempered and unfocused without his familiar. He continued the spell, pausing for the final eleven symbols to correct the incantation. Fix what he'd broken. Summon his birthright at last.

The myrtlewood staff gleamed brilliant red, the surface warm against his fingers. A fiery glow pulsed, rushing down the length of the staff and then rolling back again, turning deep orange, then gold, then white. And finally blue.

His hands shook as he took a deep breath, focusing all his concentration, and chanted the last symbols. Without a stutter or bobble.

Energy crackled, the sound like a gunshot. With tremendous force, the entire flow of magical energy contained in House Trenerry slammed into the myrtlewood staff and then Brant's body. The impact threw him across the brick stairs and onto the cold, wet ground.

Dazed, Brant laid there listening to the staff sizzle as rain misted the air and grass.

The sudden flutter of wings startled him, a deep, thrumming purr resonating across his cheek. Something brushed against his leg, beating past his stomach to hover at his shoulder.

Zip! The winged tortoiseshell cat arched her back, wings thumping the cool air as she lifted a fat, cream-colored paw to her mouth and licked it with her tiny, pink tongue.

You fixed the spell, little wizard, she said with a throaty purr between licks. *Well done.*

Brant reached out to pet the winged furball, but she slid just out of his reach.

"You did it," said Willa, kneeling beside him. "Great job, Brant! It took courage to recast that spell."

He smiled as she helped him up from the cold grass.

"I couldn't have done it without your help," he said. "And the library. How can I thank you?"

A gleam touched her deep green eyes. "Actually, you might be of some help at the library."

He raised an eyebrow. "How so?"

Willa sighed. "A testimonial on having your family grimoire digitized might go a long way with your fellow wizards."

Brant laughed. "You mean showing them it was painless and I still have the intact book?"

She nodded. "Exactly."

"Anything to help," he said. "It's the least I can do."

He reached out and stroked Zip who licked his hand then nipped it. He sighed. *Cats.*

He stepped closer to Willa, staring into her eyes as he held her hand.

"As Seattle's newest full wizard, I could give a talk reminding wizards to always um—update their spells."

Willa smiled when a white dove landed on her shoulder. Laughing, she squeezed his hand and moved closer to him.

"I'd love to discuss it over tea."

"Love to," he said, squeezing her hand.

Starfish at Ebbtide

Beware rainy nights when the beaches mist with fog
and chilly winds, sharp with brine, swirl across the cold sand. As
autumn's magic sets the forests ablaze and the oceans alight and winter's
sleep approaches, the coast becomes dangerous to mortals. Sea witches
abound and sea sprites spark against cresting waves, eager to cast curses.
And the Haystack Sentinels that tower over Oregon's coast might just
grant a wish. So, if you dare, in those darkest hours before sunrise, when
the last tide ebbs and the tide pools glisten, wish on a starfish. But make
sure you're brave enough to pay its price.

Grandma's fireside stories burned through my brain as I fastened the
top button on my jacket and wrestled black tangles of curls into a
purple scrunchie. Grandma said that locals had a healthy respect for the
Sentinels. She'd seen their magic save lives, homes, and marriages—or
destroy entire families and whole towns.

Either way, that magic was my last hope.

Wiping hot, stinging tears out of my eyes, I rushed along Cannon
Beach's dark shoreline, my green Wellington boots squishing across the
cold, storm-soaked beach. They rasped against my jeans, wool socks
hugging my calves, as I hurried toward Haystack Rock.

And the tide pools.

My cell phone jangled in my pocket, blowing up with ringtones. I ignored Mom and my two sisters' texts, half-listening for Rachel Plattan's *Fight Song* (my boyfriend, Zac's ringtone), expecting him to somehow just know what happened tonight and text me. My breath caught, heart pounding like a drum solo against my rib cage. I ached to hear the Rocky theme song blare from my pocket. Dad's ringtone. Texting me to come back to the house. Because he was home. Because he was safe.

It was long past midnight on a school night, way past when Dad should've been home from work. Like three hours way past. Instead of his deep, playful voice filling the house, there was a hollow doorbell and a subdued cop at the front door. Misty eyes focused on Mom, not my sisters and me. Stone faced. Careful, clipped words like a nail gun firing off each statement with blunt force into my chest. Right through my heart.

Ma'am, your husband, Daniel Halsted, has been in a serious car accident. *Tkat.*

Three vehicle crash...one driver pronounced dead at the scene. *Tkat, tkat.*

Three airlifted to Portland...level one trauma unit...on a respirator. *Tkat, tkat, tkat.*

I smashed my eyes closed, cold wind scouring away the tears, lips salty as I reached into my jacket pocket and switched my phone to vibrate. For a moment, I stared at the crisp black tattoo marking my index finger with a tiny infinity symbol. Just like Zac's—I couldn't help smiling. Our little secret. Hope Mom didn't notice it any time soon.

Sand crunched as I kicked sea foam out of my path, heart aching as Haystack Rock loomed dark and misty over the windy beach.

Just got my driver's license. Today. Of all days. Thanks, life! Been waiting all day for Dad to come home so I could show it to him. I brushed my sleeve across my face, wiping away a new flood of tears.

To thank him for suffering through my learning to drive. Terrified lane changes. Thousand-point parallel parking maneuvers. *Safely*, he'd say in a quiet, calm voice, never yelling. Even when I almost sideswiped a Land Rover on I-5. *Safely, Em.*

I traced the outline of my new driver's license in my pocket beside the pearl sweater pin Grandma gave me before she died last year. It was her mother's. Losing Grandma broke my heart into a million pieces. I wouldn't lose my dad, too.

Not now. Not like this.

Ahead, a silvery crescent moon gleamed through the fog, illuminating the Haystack monolith, so stark and massive against the long ribbon of silver-lit sand and dark swath of churning ocean.

A mournful fog horn called out for an answer as the frothy tide ebbed, revealing rocky tide pools swirling around the Haystack.

Grandma said that call was the Cannon Beach Sentinel, forever separated from her lover to the south, calling out to him on the tides. Yearning to hear his voice. His answer. Grandma said they were human once. Desperate for a wish, but it carried a terrible price. A curse. They had magic to grant wishes, but only when autumn turned to winter.

Silly kid's stories, but I was out of options. I had to take the risk. To save my dad.

"Emma," whispered an unfamiliar voice across the mist.

I turned, my breath sharp in the rainy chill. Not a single light shone from the endless row of dark beach houses overlooking the ocean, windows pearly black against empty footpaths winding down grassy hillsides toward the beach.

I stepped over sand dollars and ruffled kelp streamers, Wellies kicking up frothy sea foam as my name echoed again across the waves until I reached Haystack Rock's craggy, barnacled outer rocks. The huge basalt sea stack glimmered with strange gold light.

Stepping over a tide pool with dozens of tiny, light green anemones, I moved around the Haystack's larger rocks, avoiding the endless clusters of razor-sharp gooseneck barnacles. They gleamed, awash in electric purple light that danced across the rocks.

The Sentinel—she was here. I felt her presence in the fog.

Ahead, a large tide pool shimmered, water alight with a serene aqua glow that lit up Haystack Rock, ethereal lights glittering as bright as fireworks.

"Emma Halsted," called the female voice.

Dewy air glistened, a translucent form coalescing out of the rock. Flickering with human form.

She stood at least six feet tall, maybe taller. Long, wavy hair the color of sea foam flowed around her oval face, skin a pale, dusty aqua as she turned toward me, her stormy, moon-bright eyes turbulent with emotions I couldn't read. An ocean swell rose around her and then receded, water falling into a luminous blue gown at her shoulders, around her hips. Barefoot, she walked toward me, gown pulsating with stars as she stretched out her arms, fingers splayed and sparkling with sea spray.

The Sentinel.

I couldn't speak. Grandma's stories were true.

I just stood there staring at the Sentinel's bright face and the ocean's light bathing Haystack Rock and its surrounding tide pools. From the dark shore, the mist contained all of it, cradled it in sand and light and the gentle whisper of waves.

"You've come for a wish," said the lithe woman in a fluid voice that melted on the air like spun sugar.

Who or what was she? An apparition? Part of the mist? Something my aching heart conjured to save my dad. And his chances were slipping away.

I nodded, my heart pounding into my throat, tears blinding my swollen eyes. Grandma said the Sentinel had been human once. Maybe she'd understand?

The Sentinel frowned, rubbing her forehead. "There is so much noise." She pointed toward my hip. "From there. In your pocket. Clear it. It hurts my head."

I pulled my phone out of my jacket pocket, screen awash in text messages. My sisters, Liv and Taylor, filled the first screen as I swiped through the messages, flicking past Liv's six *wru wtf* texts and Taylor's string of *cm pls wru* texts. None from Zac. Not sure why. But Mom's texts went right through me.

> Emma where are you? On the way w/dad to
> hospital Liv n Tay otw too W R U?
>
> Em, turn on your phone!
>
> Answer my texts! Your Dad's bad. Don't
> want to tell you all this in a text.

> Em. Call me. Now.

> Dad's critical. He's on a respirator. Emma, don't make me do this thru texts call

> me back! We need you here!

> Emma. There's not much time. You have to get here. Now. To say goodbye.

"It's my dad...see, he's—" My voice broke. I looked away, turning off my phone.

It was almost too late, didn't she understand?

The Sentinel let out a breath. "Yes, I see it. I can focus now."

A fog horn bellowed across the ocean, cutting through the fog. The Sentinel turned toward the sound, looking south, the corners of her lips lifting into a smile. She sang a clear alto note that lamented through the mist, the tide carrying off her message.

The Sentinel's unblinking gaze settled on me again. With my eyeliner smeared, nose running, tears leaking down my face, I was a scary mess. She studied me for a few more long, awkward moments and then bent down, brushing her fingers across a shallow tide pool beside her.

"He is here," she said as images rushed across the tide pool's mirror-like surface. "Look."

Several, green interstate signs rushed past, one of them read Hillsboro as Dad's black Honda Pilot passed underneath, moving with highway traffic toward the sun hanging low on the horizon.

He looked so GQ in his grey suit and purple tie, salty black hair clipped close on the sides, longer on top, side part. He tapped his gold wedding band against the steering wheel in time to some old Bruce Springsteen CD I gave him for Father's Day. The one Liv hated and I loved.

Grinning through my tears, I nodded. "That's my dad."

I laughed, remembering him saying how he preferred his old fogie albums to discs and those new-fangled pod players (as he called them) because the sound quality was better. Until I explained that he could carry his entire music collection on one device—or stream everything from the cloud.

What happens if it's sunny and not cloudy, he'd asked me, straight-faced at the dinner table. *Does all the music disappear?*

Really, Dad? I rolled my eyes at him as his infectious laugh filled the house. He shared a private wink with Mom while Liv stared at her phone, ignoring everything now that she was in college. He laughed again when Taylor insisted on a stretch Prius limo for her prom in four years. For the environment.

Images flickered across the tide pool, panning across the highway median to a little red coupe heading toward Portland in the left-hand lane. Everything looked normal until the coupe tried to switch lanes, swerved back at the last minute, overcorrecting, and then accelerated across the median into oncoming traffic going west.

Toward the coast.

I winced, my whole body jolting as the red coupe struck Dad's Honda Pilot head on, tossing him into the right lane. Into the path of a white pickup truck.

The tide pool went dark, water swirling until a hospital ICU appeared.

Face bandaged, Dad lay in a hospital bed surrounded by dozens of monitors, hospital staff buzzing around him. Perched on his bandaged face was some sort of mask and tubing, mechanical whoosh and click of a machine beside him. I looked away, the sounds making my skin crawl.

The machine was breathing for him. Breathing for my dad.

"No...NO!" Tears flooded my face as I took a step backward. This wasn't real. This wasn't happening. None of it.

"There's more," said the Sentinel. She ran her index finger through the image, stirring it until the view widened. "Two in the white truck."

In the next room lay two young men, faces bandaged, bodies braced, casts wrapping legs and arms.

I leaned forward, trying to see their faces. Couldn't.

"Who are they?" I asked, watching the Sentinel's expression.

Her moon-bright eyes dimmed a little, sea spray misting her face.

"I've seen many things along this coast." She walked around the handful of shallow tide pools at her feet, motioning toward the nearby homes. "Generations of you repeat yesterday's mistakes, take stupid chances, refuse help. Leaving behind confused and grieving survivors who brave the fog and chill to make a wish—and weather its price."

She was beside me now, compassion in her eyes as she touched my cheek, her skin smooth and cool like the underside of my pillow when I flipped it over in the middle of the night. In a moment, her hand fell to her side and she walked away from me, back toward the rocks.

"Let's begin then."

She summoned an ocean wave that rose above her head in a sparkling arc, flowing around her into a chair. A throne. She snapped her fingers and the wave froze in place, in mid-swell. The Sentinel sat down on the frozen wave, leaning back against its translucent surface, elbows propped against sea foam arm rests.

The Sentinel sang a haunting soprano melody that lit the surf with eerie aqua brilliance. As her final note floated ashore, tiny purple and orange lights twinkled like fireflies across the sand and tide pools.

Clusters of green anemones glowed as tiny purple crabs skittered along the sand in glowing trails of light. I leaned closer, mesmerized by the glossy starfish molded like colored clay along the craggy sides of rocks. Dozens of vibrant purple starfish covered the rocks, a handful of brilliant red ones draped over rich brown ones. A single orange starfish pulsed with electric light, a bright flame against the water's luminous aqua glow.

"How did you know to come here?" the Sentinel asked.

Retrieving Grandma's pearl pin from my pocket, her last gift to me, I held it out to the Sentinel. It was my most prized possession.

"Grandma Viv told me stories about the Sentinels' magic and wishing on starfish at ebbtide," I said, the silver pearl pin cold against my bare hand.

The Sentinel smiled, her eyes misting as she ran her finger across the pearl pin. "Grandma Viv." She studied the pin in silence, her expression faraway. Finally, she looked at me. "Granting a wish has a price. What will you pay for this wish?"

"I can pay you," I said. "I have almost a thousand dollars in my savings account. And Grandma's pin. It means so much to me."

The Sentinel's expression was like granite, a wave of her hand setting images in motion across the tide pool.

"So you think a bauble will pay for a human life?"

Her tone made my heart sink into my stomach as I watched watery images of the ICU.

"It's all I have."

"Is it?" the Sentinel asked, shaking her head. "Grandma Viv didn't explain very well, did she?"

I just shrugged.

"Only a true sacrifice can pay for this kind of wish." The Sentinel leaned forward, studying my face.

She moved toward the images playing across the clear water. With a flick of her index finger, a watery doorway rose from the tide pool, beckoning me forward. She took hold of my arm and together, we walked through the glistening doorway.

Blips and beeps mixed with the steady murmur of voices as the world became scalding white chaos. Held back by medical skill and a little luck. Click of shoes against white tile floors, flurry of nurses, doctors, and paramedics ebbing and flowing through the white and glass space. Stinging scent of germicide. Flashes of color—like starfish in a tide pool—softened the whiteness: blue scrubs, red, purple, and green.

As the door closed behind us, the hospital ICU ward came into sharp glaring focus against the roar of noise. Dazed, I hung in the doorway of my dad's room, staring at the jumble of monitors and tangle of people keeping him alive.

From that doorway, I felt his distance. My heart twisted into a knot. He was leaving.

The Sentinel's tug on my jacket startled me. She pulled me away from him, through the wall, toward the two people in the white truck.

I floated beside the bed of the man on my left.

"Blood pressure's falling," said a nurse beside him.

Beneath the swelling, bandages, and braces, his tanned hand poked out from underneath the white sheet. My heart shattered as a tiny black tattoo came into focus. An infinity symbol. On his left index finger.

A sob broke through my silence as I stared at my left hand, at my own tiny infinity symbol glaring back from my index finger.

Zac! I couldn't breathe. That's why he hadn't texted me tonight.

"No!" I shouted at the Sentinel as an alarm screeched. "No! You're tricking me!"

"He's coding," said a nurse in green scrubs, others moving toward the bed.

The Sentinel pulled me out of the room as the ICU team went to work on Zac. She pushed me toward the dark, watery doorway—away from Zac—and I couldn't move.

I couldn't stop her.

Zac, my eighteen-year-old boyfriend. My love. My world. My infinity. Was dying just like my dad.

And I could only make one wish.

FOR WHAT FELT LIKE A LIFETIME, I LAY IN THE SAND BESIDE the tide pool, vivid orange starfish an arm's reach from me, fog thick, wind wild—the tide still out. I only had until the last ebbtide to make my wish. And pay its price.

One wish. Dad or my boyfriend. Make no wish and I lose them both.

The Sentinel sang to the lonesome, alto notes echoing across the mist from the south (her lover) and I couldn't help but wonder what she said to him.

Was she enjoying this moment? Separating other lovers to ease her own pain? I wanted to shout my rage across the beach and its winding footpaths, shattering every dark window. I came here to save my dad, not to lose my boyfriend. Much less make such a horrible choice.

"Time's fleeting, Emma," said the Sentinel, pacing around the tide pools. "Make your wish while you still can."

"And the price?" I demanded.

"A wish on an outgoing tide must bring something of equal weight ashore when it returns."

I lifted my head from the sand, staring into the pool's mirror calm as tears funneled down my face. This wish—and its price—would break my heart into a million shards. I glared at the infinity symbol so stark against the glimmering lights. Mocking me.

Infinity. Zac and I got these tattooed a month ago, pledging a lifetime together. Infinity lasted a month. Thirty lousy days.

I hated the Sentinel! I was glad she was trapped in stone, missing her lover. I smashed my hands against my face. I couldn't make this choice—couldn't pay this heinous price!

"All I have to give is my love for Zac," I said, glaring at her. "Like you don't know that."

"Hurry, Emma. Make the wish."

Shaking with grief, I pressed my hand against the cold, lumpy orange starfish.

"Please," I whispered. "Save my dad."

"And the price?" the Sentinel asked.

"My love for Zac," I said, my voice breaking, the words a blade through my heart. "My relationship."

"Are you certain?" the Sentinel asked. "I'll only ask you once."

I held my breath, the starfish icy against my hand.

I was giving up fourteen months of loving my Zac: celebrating with him when he won State in swimming, crying with him in my arms at his mom's breast cancer diagnosis, grieving together when Grandma Viv died. Giving each other our v-cards.

He was my best friend. My first and last thought of the day. How did I give up one of the best parts of my life? I smashed my eyes closed, trembling now.

How could I look into his eyes without seeing my dad's death?

"Yes," I said with a hiss, tears dripping across my lips and down my chin. "I hate you."

The orange starfish burst into flame, writhing into an orange fireball that shot across the night sky in a shower of sparks.

In a flash, the Sentinel disappeared and Haystack Rock went dark as fog thickened across the now-dark beach.

The infinity symbol on my index finger ignited in blue fire, roiling across the sharp black ink, turning it to ash as my memories of Zac began to disappear, ash mixing with tears that trickled like black ink down my fingers. Pooling on the outgoing tide.

Kissing behind the bleachers at his swim meets, smell of chlorine against his warm, buttery skin. Holding me up as they lowered Grandma's coffin into the ground, Zac's silky voice soothing like my favorite jeans fresh from the dryer. Making love in a tent under the stars, his heart beating against mine as he said I love you, wild rhythms entwining like the flutter of kite strings on a windy Oregon beach.

Memories, sensations—moments—ebbing with the tide as my heart shriveled into a smoldering ball of pain.

Exhausted and heartsick, I wrapped my arms around my knees, pressing my face into my sleeve, and cried. For what seemed like hours, sand clinging to my face and hair, waves lapping at my boots. Dark sky growing lighter.

Until the tide began fluttering in like feathers against the cold sand.

***

"Em, don't try to move. I've got you."

Dad's frightened face hung over me, the sky a pale blue-grey.

I stared up at him, my face twisting into an anguished mask, fresh, hot tears spewing down my face again. Saving my dad at the price of my boyfriend was too much. I wanted to die.

"You've been out here all night. Mom and I have been worried sick."

A red fleece blanket enfolded me, my teeth chattering so I hard I thought they'd break as Dad lifted me from the cold, wet sand and ran with me toward the house.

Inside, it didn't take long for my numb skin to turn to fire as Mom and Liv peeled off my cold, soaked clothes and wrapped me in blankets. Everything burned and ached as my half-frozen body began to warm up.

Dad was beside me on the burgundy couch, stroking my kelp-encrusted black curls as he wrapped me in another blanket and set a warm mug of hot chocolate with a motherload of marshmallows on top of the table. His mouth quivered as he pulled me into another hug, pressing his face into my sandy, salted hair. He smelled like cold and sweat. The house's sunny yellow walls, oak floors, and red-brick fireplace felt drafty. Empty. Despite my family crowding around me.

"Why didn't you answer our texts?" Dad asked in a quivering voice. "I've been searching for you all night, Em."

Liv leaned against the doorway, staring at her phone. She glanced over at me through dark curly bangs and rolled her eyes. "You're the obedient daughter, remember? I'm the one who gets in trouble for staying out all night," she said and returned to her phone.

I just cried on Dad's shoulder, hating myself for what I'd done. What I'd lost—no, given up.

"Here, Emma," said Taylor, patting my leg. Slinging a long lock of black hair off her shoulder, she handed me my cell phone in its turquoise paisley case, blue cable trailing off it. "I plugged in your charger for you." Taylor being her helpful, caring self.

My phone was filled with dozens of text messages. It vibrated twice in my hand and I glanced at the screen, expecting a text from Zac. But I'd given him up. I sucked in a breath. I'd never see another text from him again. I stared at my index finger, the infinity symbol gone now. Like Zac.

I threw my arms around Dad, burying my face against his chest.

Oh, Zac—it hurts so bad.

"Everything's gonna be okay, Em," said Dad, rubbing my shoulders. "I'm fine. It was just a horrible, random accident."

Accident? I sat up, staring at him. *What accident? Hadn't my wish erased the accident? Did Zac and his brother still die?*

"How'd it happen, Dad?" Taylor asked.

I held my breath.

"Car jumped the median and collided with a white pickup truck. I think you know one of them, Em. They both went to your school."

I nodded.

"Missed me by an inch," Dad continued, holding up thumb and index finger. "Hit the truck. When I got to the truck, the younger brother—curly blond haired one—had a major artery bleed."

I gasped—Zac!

"The other brother was in bad shape, too. Conscious, but trapped in the truck."

Cooper, Zac's oldest brother. I pulled away, anxious to hear the rest.

"I tied off the bleed," said Dad, staring at his hands now. "Kept him from bleeding out until the paramedics arrived. Doctor said he'd have died quick if I hadn't been there. Good thing I was there."

My heart hammered in my throat. Zac would have died if—the realization hit me like a truck—if Dad hadn't been there. If I'd chosen Zac, I'd have lost Dad and Zac both. Even if he couldn't be part of my life anymore, at least he was still here.

It still hurt, but I smiled.

"Life's a precious gift, Emma," the Sentinel whispered in my ear.

My phone lit up, a text message scrolling across the screen. From the Sentinel?

Sometimes saving it comes at a terrible price. Like a desperate mother begging a wish from a sea witch—at a terrible price.

What was the wish, I texted.

Saving my daughter, the Sentinel texted. To heal her, I had to give up what I loved the most. Being her mother. Healing her required me to give her up. But I didn't know the magic was cursed, that it would separate my husband and me for eternity. In stone.

My heart sank, a chill shuddering through my chest. Had I been cursed, too?

I'm sorry, I typed. Have I been cursed, too?

I gave you a piece of myself to protect you from the curse.

I shook my head, typing, I don't understand. Why wouldn't you just escape?

Because my daughter loved you. My daughter, Viviana. Your grandmother, Em.

What? I typed. You're my great-grandmother??? What did you give me??

Yes, Em. Viviana's pin was forged with my magic, the pearl spun from it and the songs I sing every night across the water. To my husband and my daughter. Viviana carried the pin for a long time—until she gave it to you.

What is the pearl? I typed back to her.

The most powerful magic I possess—my love. Love never dies. When you free it on the tide, it washes ashore again.

My heart twisted into a knot. The Sentinel had been trying to help me all along. She—and Grandma Viv—taught me a lesson about love I'd never forget. Someday, when the pain of losing Zac wasn't so raw, maybe I'd be able to love someone again.

I wiped tears from my eyes and rose from the couch. The landline rang. Taylor answered it and handed it to Dad.

"Yes, this is he," said Dad, pacing, cordless receiver pressed against his ear. "So glad to hear that. Glad you'll both be all right...yes, I'm fine. Just fine. Uh huh...yes. Oh, yes, of course."

Dad handed the receiver to me.

I frowned, putting it to my ear. "Hello?"

"Uh, hi—this is Zac Riley. We go to Hamilton together."

Chills danced along my skin, my heart beating so fast I thought it'd explode. Zac, my beautiful, goofy, amazing Zac! I bit my lip.

"Yes, of course, I remember you. I've seen you swim a million times."

"You have?" he said.

God, I sound like a total creeper now. "My friend, Ava's on the swim team."

"So, when I realized it was your dad who saved Coop and me, I wanted to uh, see if we could hang out sometime."

"I'd love to, Zac," I said to him, feeling the shards of my heart rasp against each other, drawing back together.

As Zac's voice thrummed in my ear, I heard ocean waves crash onto the shore, the tide returning, the Sentinel's song in my ear. Loving. Forgiving.

NOVELS BY LISA SILVERTHORNE

Standalones:

ISABEL'S TEARS

LANDFALL

PACIFIC BLUE TATTOO

A Game of Lost Souls series:

THE CINDERELLA HOUR

THE PRINCE CHARMING HOUR

THE EVER AFTER HOUR

THE FALLEN HEARTS SEASON

THE RISING SPIRITS SEASON

THE ETERNAL SOULS SEASON

THE ROYAL WEDDING HOUR

THE HEAVENLY HONEYMOON HOUR

THE DIVINE NEWLYWEDS SHOW

THE CELESTIAL COUPLES SHOW

Haunted Portraits series:

BEAUTY: CAPTURED AND FRAMED

SCIENCE FICTION WRITING AS L.S. SILVERTHORNE

Standalones:

REDISCOVERY

Experiencing True Purple series:

RECOMBINANT, Book 1

HELIX, Book 2

SHORT STORY COLLECTIONS

The Sound of Angels

The Magic of Ordinary Things

FORTHCOMING

A Game of Lost Souls series:

The Enochian Apocalypse Show, Book Eleven

The Angelic Anniversary Hour, Book Twelve

A Game of Lost Souls—Angelic Hearts:

Muriel's Spark

Kesien's Fire

Anahera's Flame

Azrael's Embers

SCIENCE FICTION WRITING AS **L.S.** SILVERTHORNE

Experiencing True Purple series:

Splice, Book 3

Cipher, Book 4

Renascence, Book 5

About the Author

LISA SILVERTHORNE has published nearly twenty novels and nearly 150 short stories and novelettes in many genres. Her short fiction has appeared in professional publications that include: DAW Books, Roc Books, *Pulphouse Magazine*, *Fiction River,* Wildside Press, and Prime Books. She lives in Las Vegas, Nevada.

www.ingramcontent.com/pod-product-compliance
Lightning Source LLC
Chambersburg PA
CBHW061923220726
48287CB00018B/823